SAM CRESCENT

EVERNIGHT PUBLISHING ®

www.evernightpublishing.com

Copyright© 2016

Sam Crescent

Editor: Karyn White

Cover Artist: Sour Cherry Designs

Jacket Design: Jay Aheer

ISBN: 978-1-77233-987-1

SAM CRESCENT

FEAR THE BOSS

Deadly Duet, 1

Sam Crescent

Copyright © 2014

Chapter One

Caleb Cassell wiped his bloody hands on the cloth one of his men handed to him. The sound of screams filled the abandoned warehouse he owned. Once his hands were free of blood he grabbed his cell phone to see if there were any calls waiting for him. Seeing three from the women he kept on a regular basis for sex, he deleted them all, turning back to see if his right hand man and partner, Henry, had gotten the information he needed.

"Please, make it stop," John, the man bound to the chair, said, whimpering.

Folding his arms, Caleb was bored. Why did little shits really think they could mess with him? At thirty-five years old he'd proven to all of the rival gangs that he wasn't to be messed with. He owned girls, drugs, and money. Over the years he'd proven more than once that he wasn't afraid of killing his enemies, or at the least torturing them first. Caleb kept a firm hold on everything, making sure no one fucked with him. He wasn't a cruel man to people who followed the rules, and he was fair to everyone who was honest with him. Those people who broke the rules and tested him, were then hurt. Caleb did warn all of them before he hired anyone.

The front of all of his businesses was his nightclubs. No one looked too closely unless someone died on his property from the drugs taken. Most of the time, Caleb got men to dump the body elsewhere. He'd grown up on the streets and knew how the people worked. When there was an economic downturn people sought him out for money, work, or drugs to forget all about the world.

"Where is the money from the drugs, John? I'm not in the mood for your shit," Caleb said, still feeling bored.

John whimpered, crying out as Henry grabbed his hair, yanking his head back.

Blood dripped from John's lip, head, and nose. His face was black and blue from his and Henry's punishments. Caleb was bored. He hated dealing with addicts, and from the track marks on John's arms, the man was a fucking user.

Not only had he used product that Caleb intended to sell, he'd taken money by also dealing the shit within his club.

"Please, I'm sorry. I'll make it back, boss," John said, wheezing.

It would be more work to take John to the hospital, and then if he squealed to the cops, the work and payoff would be too much money.

"No, you won't make it back. There's nothing you can do." Caleb turned to look at Henry. "Kill him and dispose of the body. I'm done with this piece of shit."

John started to scream and whimper before Caleb had even left the building.

Spinning on his heel, he walked outside as the bullet rang out. Pulling out the packet of cigarettes, he took out a smoke and lit it. Inhaling the nicotine he stared up at the night sky contemplating which bitch he was going to take for the night. Providing he had a lot of money, any woman came to his need. He was never short of a whore to put his dick inside. All women were whores; it's what he was taught on the streets. He had yet to meet a woman who was worth more than a passing glance. Sure, the women he dated were beautiful, but they'd been with a lot of men, making them a little too bitter to the world.

Henry walked out, talking on the phone as he went.

"The disposal team?" Caleb asked once Henry hung up.

"Yeah, we've got to wait for them to arrive. You got a couple of grand on you to pay them?"

Nodding, Caleb went to the trunk of the car. Flicking the lock, he opened it up and peeled away the carpet to reveal the small safe he kept hidden. "I've got plenty of cash."

Henry lit up a smoke and leaned against the car. "He pissed himself again."

"Fucker knew he'd done wrong. I'd be more surprised if he didn't." Blowing out a ring, Caleb listened to the passing city life. He loved living in the city. There were so many people waiting to plunge down that slippery spiral of life.

"What are you doing for the rest of the night? Henry asked.

Caleb had met Henry over ten years ago. They'd been fighting for the same side in the underground fighting ring. Both of them were vicious and had been trained by the same man. After a year of playing the circuit they had both gone out to make a living for themselves. Now, they were a team, but most of the business was down to Caleb. Henry had a large scar down the side of his face from a fight gone wrong. His face put off prospective business partners. They learned long ago that Caleb handled the business while Henry was the muscle. When it was between them, they were friends. Caleb would die to save Henry, and he knew the other man was the same.

Their friendship was the only thing Caleb actually cared about. The money just made life easier, and fucking was fun while it lasted. His friendship with Henry was cemented. They were a team.

"I was going to meet Tiffany, but the bitch is too busy pissing me off. She wants something more, so I got to stop by the jewelry store and pick her something up. I may fuck her before I give her the present."

"Cold, boss. Women like being wined and dined."

"Don't have the time. I don't give a fuck about a good meal. If I wanted that, I'd get takeout at a restaurant. The only thing I need is a good woman to make me happy for a couple of hours." He threw his smoke on the ground and stubbed it out with his foot. "Stop calling me boss."

"It's easier to call you that. I'm used to it now. We both know we've only gotten this far because of you. I don't know shit about numbers or business. I can fight. That's all I'm good for."

Caleb didn't argue with him. Within the hour the cleaning crew arrived. He dealt with the money and stayed until the body was safely out of his warehouse.

Climbing into the car, he waited for Henry to drive away.

"Where we going?"

"Take me to the jewelry store you use." Caleb rubbed at his temples feeling the need for some sleep. First, he needed to fuck someone. Tiffany he'd fuck and then dump. It would be far easier that way to get what he wanted.

"You go through a lot of women," Henry said.

"Last I checked you were fucking all the whores that work at the club." Within his many nightclubs Caleb also supplied a lot of women for the men looking for some action. He didn't force them, and he made sure they got a good cut of their income. In the beginning he was running the club, doing drugs on the side, and then some women approached him. He couldn't believe a group of women actually came to him for protection so they could conduct their business.

"Hey, they give me what I need, and I give them what they need."

Shaking his head, Caleb chuckled. "Can you believe we were just fighters over a decade ago?"

"No, I can't, but I sure as fuck feel it sometimes. My body knows it has been a punching bag to one too many fuckers," Henry complained, opening and closing his hand into a fist.

"I know what you mean."

Caleb had many scars over his body from fighters who'd pulled a knife on him. Even though underground fighting had rules it didn't stop men from pulling out a knife.

"Still, I'd rather be living this life than working the circuit like a lot of young men. At least we've got a choice who we pummel," Henry said.

"Sure."

Henry pulled up outside of the jewelry store. Climbing out of the car, Caleb headed inside. Glancing behind him, he saw Henry resting on the hood of the car, lighting up another smoke. "Are you coming in?"

"I don't need pretty shit to get what I want. I'll wait here."

Not bothering to argue with the man, Caleb entered the small store. He used the same place all the time to buy his gifts. Most of the time he sent one of the waitresses at the club to get him what he needed and rarely came out to buy shit. Tonight was important. After a quick roll in the sack, he didn't want to have to be dealing with the bitch again.

Once inside, he saw there were only two women on staff. The brunette was talking to a young couple. From the look of them they were getting engaged.

The blonde he spotted long before the brunette. She was polishing the glass on the display case. Her long blonde hair caressed the top of her ass as it cascaded down her back. She wore the same blue uniform as the other woman, and the skirt ended at her knees. The view of her back showed her to be on the plump side, but Caleb always did have a thing for blondes. Both women were not overly slender, but the blonde was rounder than the brunette. He'd not seen her face yet, but if she repulsed him, he could always put a bag over her head.

Maybe the night wasn't going to be so bad after all.

****

Donna Smith tried not to chuckle as the man buying an engagement ring was trying to go for the cheapest option while also appearing to be more loving than anyone else. She'd been working in the jewelry store, Dreams, for the last year. Over that year she'd seen so many couples coming in and arguing over the kind of ring they deserved. The cost of the rings in Dreams was too expensive. She'd never be able to afford an item even though she worked here. The pay was okay, better than a lot of places, but not perfect.

She bent down and rubbed at the glass. The only problem with customers was they touched the glass. They didn't need to touch the glass to see items, yet they all did.

Someone cleared his throat right behind her. Standing up, she turned to see a male customer staring at her. His eyes were dark brown, almost black. Frowning, she glanced over his shoulder to see Lydia was busy.

"Can I help you?" she asked.

He kept staring at her. Keeping her gaze on his, she waited for him to start speaking. Holding the can of polish in one hand and a cloth in the other, she didn't have any other option other than to stare back at him. Still, he didn't say anything.

Frowning, she wondered what the hell to do.

"Can I help you?" She repeated the question in case he didn't hear her the first time.

"Yes, you can. I'm looking for a piece of jewelry for a woman."

"Okay." She stepped around him, placing the cleaning products on the nearest counter. Rubbing her hands down her uniform she turned back toward him, plastering a smile on her face. "The lady you're buying for, is she a fiancée, sister, daughter?"

"None of the above."

"Erm, what are you hoping to get from the piece?" she asked. It was easier to know the intention of the gift so she could help him pick.

"I want a parting gift that's expensive enough that she won't cause me problems."

Wow, okay, she'd never heard anything like this.

"We've got necklaces, earrings, bracelets." She stepped forward toward the window. Putting on her professional face, she pointed out different designs. He kept nodded at her talk and stood far too close to her.

More often than not she bumped into him and had to apologize. The couple who were inside had long gone.

Lydia kept glancing her way. They were getting close to packing away for the night. The night shift was always the hardest. There was a higher chance of being robbed at night than during the day. Donna always carried her pepper spray just in case someone decided to attack her.

"Can I see that one in the back?" he asked.

"Sure." Moving away from him, she went to Lydia for an excuse to be away from his closeness.

"What are you doing?" Lydia asked.

"Can I have your keys? I don't want to be too close to him." He unnerved her with his lack of talking and closeness.

"You've got a set attached to your hip."

"I know, but I needed to come away."

"Do you want me to finish serving him?" Lydia asked.

Donna nodded. "If you wouldn't mind?"

"I don't mind."

Lydia went to the man while Donna finished signing up the till. She went through the charts, and seconds later Lydia walked back. "You've got to go and serve him. He doesn't want any other woman but you to serve him. Unless you don't want the sale then you're out of luck."

Gritting her teeth, she walked back toward him. She grabbed the keys from her hip and opened up the door. Retrieving the case with the gold bracelet on, she showed it to him.

"Do you have a problem with me?" he asked.

"No."

"Then why did you send her over?"

"Lydia is better when it comes to the discussion of the pieces. I'm not particularly good." She didn't look into his eyes. "This is a really good piece. Delicate but intricate." She placed the case on the far counter and offered him up the jewelry.

He glanced over it. His large hands turned the item this way and that. She noticed his knuckles looked a little bruised.

With the business suit she didn't imagine him having anything wrong or out of place. The bruised knuckles were out of place.

"Yes, I like this one. I'll take it."

Taking the piece from his hands she touched his skin and glanced up. His gaze was on hers. He seemed to see more than what was there.

"Do you have a boyfriend or husband?" he asked.

"That's none of your business." Putting the case away, she stepped away from him, shocked by his penetrating gaze. She wasn't a beauty, not by a long stretch. When men came into the shop they were all over Lydia, not her.

Moving behind the desk, she glanced back at him. "Do you want it gift wrapped?" she asked.

"Yes." He placed his hand on the counter, and she couldn't help but look at his hands. The bruises looked painful.

"Do you want to go out with me?" he asked.

Jerking her gaze back up to his, she saw he hadn't taken his eyes off her.

"No," she said, shaking her head.

"What?"

"No, I don't want to go out with you."

She finished packing up his bracelet and ran the amount into the till. He shocked her by paying with cash. The man counted every single note onto the counter.

Watching the money pile up, she took it from the shelf and placed it in the till, handing him a receipt.

"Do you work here often?" he asked.

"Yes. Do you want to know when my manager gets in?"

Was he going to complain about her? He was acting way too creepy to be nice to.

"No. I was wondering when you were here. I'll be seeing you, Donna."

His gaze caressed over her name tag over her breast. There was something strange about him. The bell went letting her know he was gone.

"Was it me, or was he a little strange?" Lydia asked, coming up behind her.

"Yeah, he was creepy. Scary, creepy guy. We should nickname him that from now on." Donna's hands were shaking from the interaction. What was his problem?

She worked with Lydia, and they both locked up the store, securing the safety guards in place on their way out.

"Do you want a lift to your apartment?" Lydia asked.

"Nah, I'll walk. It's out of your way anyway."

"I'd hate to be walking the city streets this late at night."

"It's no problem for me. I'll see you tomorrow."

"You certainly will. The bills are not going to pay themselves." Lydia waved to her, and she watched the other woman leave before going into her bag to grab her pepper spray. Wrapping her jacket around her body she started the short walk to her apartment block. The walk wasn't the problem. What she hated the most was the dark alleys she had to pass that hid men from her sight.

Her thoughts returned to the strange customer. What had he been hoping to achieve? She never got personal with a customer. Lydia a few months back had gotten a lot of stick from a customer, a married man who thought there was more between them than a simple customer relationship.

Donna had no intention of being hurt by a guy she didn't know.

The moment she was outside of her apartment block, she ran up the stairs. The block wasn't too bad, but she didn't trust the shadows. Women could be attacked anywhere from not being cautious. Taking her keys out of her bag, she slid the key into the lock and entered her apartment. Flicking the light on, she was greeted by Pearl, her cat. She'd found Pearl as a kitten wandering around outside. She couldn't allow anything bad to happen to the poor kitten, and she'd taken her inside. It was a female kitten.

"Hey, Pearl, did you miss me?" She bent down to stroke her back. "Yeah, I missed you, too."

Picking up her cat, she dropped her bag to the floor then walked into the kitchen. Her cat purred as she started to buzz around the kitchen.

"I met a strange man today. Yes, I did."

She always talked to her cat even when she had nothing to talk about. Making herself a cup of tea, she put more milk into the cat bowl then took a seat.

Putting her head in her hands, she watched her pet and thought about the mystery man. He freaked her out, and yet she couldn't deny the sudden jolt through her body their touches had created.

Chapter Two

Walking out of the jewelry store, he saw Henry was already behind the wheel. Climbing into the passenger side, Caleb looked through the window to see Lydia and Donna talking. None of the women looked toward the windows to see who was looking in.

"Do you know that blonde woman?" Caleb asked, pointing to the store.

Henry looked through the window. "The chubby girl?"

"Yeah?"

"Yes."

"I haven't got a clue who she is. Do you?"

"No." Caleb rubbed a hand down her face. "Get our guys finding out all they can on the blonde girl known as Donna. The sooner you can get everything, I want the details." Staring at his hand, Caleb wondered what the hell had happened. Going into the store, he'd had every intention of getting what he wanted then getting the hell out of there. Instead, she'd turned around to face him, and he saw the most beautiful blue eyes he'd ever seen. What was it about her? She was so sweet looking.

Not once had she given into his attempts to find more about her.

"You know how insane you sound, right?"

"I know. Get me the details on her. Offer them a ten grand reward. That's how much I want this information." Sitting back, he tapped his leg with the box containing the bracelet.

Henry pulled up outside of the club, parking in their usual spot. "Are you sure? I'll make the call now, but you've got to be sure this is what you want."

"Yes, call them. I want information. The faster they get it to me, the higher the reward will go." He entered the club leaving Henry to make the call.

The energy inside was already high. He walked straight to the VIP section. The guard, Barry, who was on duty, nodded at him and let him pass.

"Sir, Tiffany's up there, and she's been causing a few problems tonight."

"Why wasn't I informed?" Caleb asked.

"You were busy tonight. We didn't want to disturb you."

Letting out a sigh, Caleb glanced around the club. There was not a single drug in sight. If the cops were to do a raid they wouldn't find anything. His men were paid well to keep that shit out of sight and cleaned up.

"Any other problems?"

"A couple of the clients upstairs thought they could get fresh with one of the girls. The guy and his friend will not be causing any problems."

"Good. Thank you." Caleb turned away and headed toward the main room. Several customers nodded his way. They were good for business and took a good cut of the drugs he had on offer. Some of them were agents to the stars.

Caleb had learned not to ask questions and to simply supply.

He found Tiffany sprawled out on one of the chairs sipping from a glass. His anger spiked as soon as he saw the evidence of her snorting. The whole of his club was in top shape, and yet Tiffany could ruin everything by her lack of decorum.

"Hey, baby," she said, slurring her words.

Without thinking, he grabbed her arm and hauled her up against him. He was so fucking pissed off with her. Glancing toward Barry, he signaled for the man to clean the mess up.

Leading her away from the commotion, he opened the main door and climbed three flights of stairs.

"Caleb, ouch, you're hurting me," she complained, yelling for him to stop.

He didn't stop. Opening the door to his apartment within the building, he threw her on the floor.

"What the fuck do you think you're doing?" he asked.

"What? You were the one who said I could have what I wanted when I wanted it." She giggled, getting to her feet.

Caleb finally saw Tiffany for what she was. She was an addict travelling down a slippery slope into self-destruction. Not only was she causing problems for him, she was going to start causing problems for the club.

Staring at the bracelet he saw the beautiful blonde who'd served him. She was fresh and pure, away from this lifestyle. He should leave her alone.

"You're out." He threw the box at her.

"What?" she asked, staring at the box then at him.

"Get your shit, and do not come to the club again. I'm done with you."

He stepped over her, heading toward the kitchen. This was not his main apartment. He used this place to take his women. No one was allowed back to his place. He didn't permit it. The women he dated were only allowed to see this place or he went back to theirs.

"Wait, you can't do this. You need me."

"I don't need you, Tiffany. It's over. Get your shit together and get out. I'm done here." He poured himself a scotch as she started to yell, curse, and throw shit.

Henry entered the apartment ten minutes later.

"What the fuck's happening?" he asked.

"Bitch was snorting coke out in the open and thought she could get away with it. Barry is getting together a team to collect her and dispose of her." If he didn't arrive soon, Caleb was going to do something he promised himself he wouldn't do: he was going to hit a woman.

"Stupid fucking bitch."

"Yeah, tell me about it." He sipped at his scotch then moved toward Tiffany. She'd thrown several ornaments and vases across the room.

"You're a fucking bastard. Do you know that? You take a woman, get what you want, and spit her out." Tiffany lifted up a glass plate and aimed it at him. He ducked, and the plate missed him by inches.

"Are you done yet?"

"I gave you everything you wanted."

"I did the same for you. You're the one acting like I hurt you. You want to be a bitch about it, fine, be a bitch. Don't pretend you didn't know this wasn't going to last." Her body was too slender, and he found himself making comparisons to Donna.

What was it about the other woman?

Tiffany laughed. "You know what, fine. I'll go and take my shit. Maybe I'll go and have a word with Drake. He likes me."

Drake Stone was their main rival. He was a pimp, a cruel man who forced women and girls into the lifestyle after he got them hooked onto drugs.

"Tell him a few of your trade secrets. I mean, I do know stuff that you don't even know."

She ran her finger up his chest.

Gripping her wrist, he slammed her against the wall. She cried out, and he covered her mouth. With one of his hands holding her arms above her head, he used his other to cover her mouth and nose so she couldn't breathe.

"I want you to listen to me closely, slut. You go spouting shit off to Drake then you're going to end up dead. Now, you can leave this place alive, or I will end you here. I've got no problems killing you, Tiffany. You mean shit to me."

Tears leaked out of her eyes as she stared back at him. She shook her head. The panic was finally getting to her.

"You were nothing but a hole for me to enjoy." He held his hand over her mouth several seconds before he released her. She gasped for breath. "Now, what's it going to be?"

The door to the apartment opened, and he heard his men getting closer.

"I'll go. I promise I'll go."

Barry rounded the corner.

"Good. Take this piece of trash out," he said, pushing her into Barry's arms.

It didn't take long for his men to get her out of his sight.

"Fucking slut," Caleb said, walking back into the kitchen. Henry was eating a sandwich as he entered. "They're getting me information on her?"

"Yeah, they want to know how important it was. I told them the reward you were willing to give for any information they could find."

"Good." He finished off his scotch and placed it on the counter. "I guess it's going to be a lonely night for me."

"What about your other women?" Henry asked.

"I can't. I've already sent them gifts to get rid of them. Tiffany was the only one I hadn't sent anything."

"Is this because of the girl at the store?"

Caleb shook his head. "No. Women get too attached."

"I don't know, Caleb. This blonde is different."

"I asked you to get information on a woman, so what?"

Henry sighed. "You can get any woman you've ever wanted. You've never needed ground work to be done. Tiffany was more than enough, and within hours of meeting this woman, you've gotten rid of her."

"I had every intention of getting rid of her."

"I'm just saying, maybe you need to take a step back just in case." Henry held his hands up. "I don't want you to get hurt."

Nodding at his friend, Caleb waved a hand at him. "I'll see you tomorrow."

****

Donna stretched out her tired limbs. Pearl did the same, and she stroked her cat's back. "It's time to get up again. I've got the early shift this time. I'm in at nine." She stayed in bed, stroking her cat, thinking about work. The job was not the worst one she'd had. Before she worked as a sales assistant at Dreams, she'd worked in a bar, then at a diner. All the jobs had men in different states of drink. She hated working with alcohol.

Her parents had been killed by a drunk driver when she was fourteen. With no other family she had been sent into foster care. She'd been lucky as an elderly couple took her in for the last years of their life. They lived for six months after she graduated high school, and then both were killed by an infection.

That was five years ago. She didn't go to college and preferred to work. Even though she graduated she'd never really enjoyed school. There was always something missing from her life. The past five years had been lonely, but she had her cat.

There were no men in her life or boyfriends. She didn't like being around members of the opposite sex. They always made her nervous. All of her life, even when her parents were alive, she'd avoided being around men. After getting bullied over her weight when she was younger, she'd learned to keep a lot of things to herself.

"I better get up for work before they give my job to someone else." She stroked Pearl one last time then got up. She did her business in the bathroom, brushed her teeth, washed her hands, and changed into a fresh set of clothes.

Before she headed out, she made herself some toast and coffee at the same time she quickly set Pearl some food out. In no time she was back out the door and walking toward the jewelry store. There were times she felt like all she did was work.

She did enjoy taking long walks in the park, but getting the time and the weather together was hard. Lydia was already opening up the shop by the time she arrived.

"Hey, I didn't think you were going to make it inside."

"I made it. I'm here." She followed her friend inside, and they locked the door. The shop wasn't due to open for another thirty minutes.

"No problems getting home safely last night?" Lydia asked.

"No problems. You really should stop worrying about me. I'm going to be fine. More than fine." She entered the back room, put the kettle on, and set down her jacket and bag. "What about you?"

"I got home within ten minutes. I was so tired. I think it's time I started looking for another job. This one is starting to take its toll."

"Why?" Donna asked.

"The late nights and early mornings. I'm not a fan of working nights. I never have been. I'm thinking of putting my resignation in. I've just got to find another job before I leave."

Donna was disappointed. She liked Lydia, and they worked well together.

"What about you?" Lydia asked.

"What about me?"

"Are you going to be giving in your notice?"

Shaking her head, she didn't look up from stewing the tea. "I like it here. I'm not leaving anytime soon."

"Honey, there are far better jobs out there for us. Don't you hate working late and then having to come in early the next morning?"

They divided their shift with two other women who ran the shop. Both of them alternated working days.

"I don't mind. I've got nowhere else to go." Donna shrugged but offered Lydia a smile.

"Fine. When I leave I'll keep in touch, okay?"

Donna nodded even though she knew it wasn't going to be the truth. No one kept in touch once they left the old job behind.

"I'm going to go and open the shop." She left Lydia alone to open up the blinds so customers knew they were open. They were in the middle of the city, and they had so many different customers to entertain. There was a red emergency panic button underneath the till that went straight to the police. In her year of working she hadn't pressed it once.

Lydia spoke to her about the future. After the third time, Donna tuned out of the conversation concentrating on everything but what she had to say. By lunch time she was happy with the silence when Lydia went out to lunch with her current boyfriend. She didn't ask for introductions and didn't pay any attention as they left the shop. Sitting behind the desk, she took bites of her sandwich while waiting for customers to enter the store.

There were times when there were long lulls in activity. Not everyone wanted a ring or a gift.

With her lunch finished, she headed toward the back to place her containers in her bag. The bell went, and she turned only to pause when she saw the man from last night.

He closed the door and started looking around the space. When he spotted her, he stopped.

"Hello, Donna."

How did he remember her name?

"Can I help you?" she asked, rubbing her hands together. Walking behind the counter, she stared at him. He was dressed in a suit again, and she noted his knuckles were still badly bruised. "Did your lady friend not like the bracelet?"

"I imagine my lady friend is pawning that bracelet to get what she can."

There was no response for her to say.

"Erm, okay. Do you need anything else?" she asked.

"My name's Caleb."

What was going on?

His black hair was pushed off his face, but his eyes were still as dark as last night. All of her warning bells were going off like crazy, telling her to stay away from him.

"What do you want?" she asked.

"I don't know."

He kept staring at her. She started to move toward the panic button. Caleb was scaring her.

His gaze followed the movement of her hand. He reached out and stopped her from touching the panic button.

"Don't," he said. "I'm not going to hurt you."

"You're scaring me."

"I want to get to know you."

"I don't."

His fingers banded around her wrists, and she gazed down to see his slightly tanned flesh against her pale skin.

"Can't I convince you?" he asked.

"I don't know you." Why didn't she shoot him down? Why did she believe that he wasn't going to hurt her? None of her reactions toward him made any sense.

"Then let me get to know you."

He wasn't hurting her. His grip was firm yet not painful. The heat from his body was making her warm inside.

Licking her lips, she glanced down at his touch then back up at him. "Could you please let me go?"

"Don't touch the panic button and I will."

"Okay."

She'd agree to anything if he'd just let her go so she could think. His touch shouldn't do this to her. Having no control over her reactions unnerved her.

Caleb released her hand. Keeping her palms on the counter in front of her she stared at him.

"Have you heard of the club Ecstasy?"

"Yes." She'd heard of it and hated it. Why name a club after a drug? In the back of her mind, she knew the word was also used for something else, too, but she wanted to see the negative more than the positive. It was almost as if he was begging for the cops to come charging down his door.

"I own it." He reached into his pocket and handed her the card. "Come on Friday night. The drinks will be on me."

"If I come to this club will you stop arriving here?" she asked.

He nodded.

Maybe by the time Friday came he would have forgotten all about her. *Do you want him to forget about you?*

His attention was nice, flattering even, but he scared her. The suit he wore told one story while the bruises on his knuckles told another. She didn't know which story to believe about him and would rather have nothing to do with him.

"Friday?"

She nodded again.

"No, I need you to say you're coming."

"Why?"

"Because I know you'll keep your word and not go against it."

Staring at the card, shame filled her. "You don't know me."

"I know enough about people. Come to the club and I promise to leave you alone." Over his shoulder she saw Lydia enter the store. Her friend paused when she saw Caleb. "I'll go for now. You don't come Friday, then I'll come back."

"You're threatening me."

"I'm hoping you'll see it as a determination to get to know one another."

"I don't want to get to know you." The words spilled from her lips before she could stop them.

"I hope you're wrong. Give me a chance." He stepped back, and within seconds he was gone.

Staring at where he stood, she gazed down at the card.

"Wow, Donna. What did he want this time?" Lydia joined her behind the counter.

"He wants me to go to his club." She handed the card over to her friend.

Lydia took the card and whistled. "I love this place. It's a little shady, but they've got great service and drinks there. Are you going?"

"I don't know."

"Why not?"

"It's not really my scene."

"I'll go with you. Darren will come with us. That way we've got some protection." Lydia handed her back the card.

"I don't know. I'm not really into the club scene."

"From what you told me, Donna, you're not into any scene. You've not got much of a choice. He wants to get to know you, and at least this is a public place."

Seeing Lydia's point, she pocketed the card. Part of her was overjoyed about his attention while the sane part of her knew it was a mistake. There was something off about Caleb, but she just didn't know what.

Chapter Three

On Friday night Caleb was sat in the VIP area drinking a strong scotch and looking over the club. From his vantage point he saw everything and everyone. He knew a select group of girls were seated in line with the dance floor so any man who wanted some action would see them instantly. A group of men were being watched with caution as they looked dangerous to him. He'd dealt with a lot of men carrying roofies for the girls. No woman was going home or being raped by a guy she didn't want.

He had standards.

Henry threw himself down into the chair beside him. "I'm bored."

"Go and find yourself some entertainment. I've got stuff to do."

"You're waiting for the blonde."

Caleb glanced toward the door as another group entered the club. They were scantily clad women looking for action. He'd gotten the file on Donna Smith within twenty-four hours of asking for it. The reward he'd paid was over ten grand, but it was well worth the money. Every little detail, even her medical history, was down on paper for him to read. Tuesday he spent all day at his apartment reading through her file. He knew about the drunk driver who was serving time for killing her parents and about the foster parents, also dead, whom she'd lived with after the accident. She'd graduated from school at eighteen and was working within the month of their deaths. Her grades were good but not brilliant. She didn't even apply for college.

She'd changed jobs five times before getting the job at Dreams. Her employers adored her. Donna was a hard worker, and she didn't have any serious medical problems. She'd not been in the car when her parents were killed.

What he did know was the fact she wasn't on any birth control pills. There was nothing exciting about her and she didn't pose a threat to anyone, yet he couldn't get her out of his head. She was there all the time.

"This is dangerous for us, your obsession."

"I've never had an obsession, Henry. Stop worrying about it."

"It's a woman, Caleb. Fuck her already and move on. I know I will." Henry stopped a waitress to order a beer.

"If you're here to ruin my mood then please leave." He sipped his drink and then stood. "I'm going to take a leak. Try not to scare anyone away."

He walked toward the private bathroom and stared at his reflection in the mirror. Maybe he was losing his mind. There was nothing special about Donna Smith. The attraction was inside him, not her. She was a blonde, and he loved fucking blondes. Something told him she was different from all other women.

Women are whores, and you'll do well to remember that.

His fighting mentor would scream that at them whenever a groupie was near them. Women were a bunch of distractions men had to deal with. They were only good for one thing and that was being a place to stick their dick.

"You're thirty-five fucking years old. Get a fucking grip."

She was twenty-three years old. Donna was twelve years his junior and way too innocent for this lifestyle. He made deals with crooks, criminals, drug dealers, and whores while Donna didn't do anything besides work.

Running a hand down his face, he exited the bathroom and went back to sit in his chair.

"Are you done now?" Henry asked.

Shaking his glass for a refill, Caleb ignored his friend. Keeping his eye on the door, he waited for Donna to enter.

For the next thirty minutes she didn't turn up. He had her address and would go and hassle her there if it wasn't for the risk of the cops getting involved. Plenty of the police force was on his payroll, but he wasn't going to let them know of his interest in Donna.

"I guess she's not turning up, boss." Henry stood. "I'm going to test out the goods next door."

He watched Henry walk away then focused his attention on the club. Men and women were grinding together on the dance floor. Out of the corner of his eye he saw a flash of blonde hair. Standing up, he stepped closer to the rail, and there she was, sitting at the bar. She must have arrived when he went to the bathroom. Buttoning up his shirt, he saw a man was trying to talk to her.

Caleb didn't like anyone touching what was his. He paused at the sudden thought. During all of his time with his women, he'd never once been interested in who else they fucked. He used a condom and forced them to get checked at the hospital.

Walking down the steps he kept his gaze on the man.

When he was a foot away from her, he was able to hear them.

"No, really, I don't want to dance. I'm here to meet someone," Donna said. She wore a black dress, one he was sure she wore to a funeral rather than out at a club.

"Baby, I don't see anyone waiting for you. Come on, I can take you for a spin on the dance floor." He reached out to touch her.

Seeing the other man's hand on her body filled Caleb with rage. No one got to touch her but him.

Stepping up close, he grabbed the man's hand and twisted it. He didn't give a fuck if he broke the guy's wrist. Men needed to learn not to touch what was his.

"Caleb," Donna said, squeaking his name.

"I suggest you find a woman of your own and stay away from mine. This is my club, my woman."

"You're Caleb?" the man asked.

"Yes."

The fear was instant in the other man's eyes. Caleb didn't care.

"I'm gone."

"Good." He waited for the other guy to go before turning back to her.

"You didn't need to do that," she said.

"Did you want him touching you? Forgive me. I didn't think you were the kind of woman to want anyone touching her." He took a seat as she gasped.

"That was unfair and uncalled for. I'm only here because you asked me to be here." She stood up. "If all you want to do is insult me then you can do that when I'm working." She spun away.

He caught her hand and tugged her back. She fell against him, and he caught her, picking her up and placing her on her seat. "I'm not here to insult you. The bastard pissed me off thinking he could touch you."

"I refused to dance with him. I was about to pull away from him when you arrived." She clasped her hands together and averted her gaze.

"Look at me."

Her blue eyes glanced back at him.

For several seconds neither of them spoke. She was beautiful and pure. Was that the draw? In all of his years he'd never been with a woman who was pure. Was she a virgin?

None of those questions would be answered tonight. He doubted she'd even allow him to kiss her.

"I'm here. What do you want?" she asked.

What was going through that head of hers?

"I'll buy you a drink." He signaled for the waiter.

"I don't drink."

"We serve sodas here as well." He took hold of her hand and pulled her close. The club was getting busy, and he struggled to hear her. "Come on. Let's go to the VIP section." Without waiting for her response, he led her toward Barry. The guard didn't say a word as he took her past the man to the section he made sure clients paid more than her salary to get into.

She took a seat next to him, and he ordered her a soda.

"My friends are down there."

"We can see them from here. They're perfectly safe."

He noticed her hands were shaking, and she locked them together placing them in her lap.

"Why are you scared?"

She turned to look at him. "I don't know why I'm here. You come into the store for a bracelet for a woman and now you're giving me ultimatums."

"I was hoping you'd be wanting to get to know me." He leaned back in his chair to stare at her. She'd not done anything with her hair, and it simply fell around her in waves. The length was beautiful, and he imagined it was silky to the touch.

The black dress she wore did nothing for her figure. The curves he felt moments ago were hidden behind unflattering fabric. The dress fell to her calves covering her legs from view. At least the neckline showed off her cleavage showing him the full size of her tits. He was a tits and ass man. There was nothing he liked more than spanking a woman's ass and sucking on her nipples as he fucked her to completion.

His cock thickened, and he moved trying to get comfortable.

"Why?" she asked.

"Don't you want to get to know me?"

She stopped and frowned. "I've never given it much thought."

"You've never gotten to know any man, have you?"

Her cheeks heated, and he knew his answer. The woman before him was a virgin. There was no other way she'd be blushing at a simple question. He liked it even though he was shocked.

"I don't know why I'm here with you. You could have any woman you want, and yet you're here, with me."

"I want you, Donna. I'm a man used to getting what I want."

"That man earlier, the moment he mentioned your name I saw the fear in his eyes. Who are you?" she asked.

He jerked at her response. She watched and read people. Staring into her eyes, he saw the curiosity lurking there. She didn't want to get to know him yet she was intrigued by him, just like he was intrigued by her.

"Let's just say I'm not the type of man who takes crap from others."

"You're being vague on purpose."

"Sometimes, you should just accept the answer you're given," he said.

"I don't trust you," she said.

He smiled. "A lot of women don't trust their own husbands and yet they married them."

She stopped, biting her lip. "This isn't a good idea." She made to stand up, but he stopped her, placing a hand on her leg. He'd never begged a woman to stay and keep him company.

"Don't go."

"This is a waste of time. You don't know me, and I don't know you." She was itching to find any excuse to leave, and he needed to stop her.

****

"Are you so afraid to live that you'd rather push me into one box so that you can die a virgin and righteous?"

His question caught her off guard. Donna stared into his eyes and knew he was going to win whatever they had going on.

She didn't trust him, not by a long shot. There was something in the way the other man reacted that told her there was more to Caleb than he was letting on.

"You shouldn't say things like that."

"What? You're a virgin. I'm not saying anything wrong. You refuse to take a chance in life and would rather hide from everyone. I bet you even own a cat."

His assumptions about her were right on the mark.

Glaring at him, she felt her anger spike. "Have you ever considered the fact some men are not worth the time they demand? They're cruel and mean and try to change the women they want to be with."

"Just like women do with men."

She'd not dated men as the disappointment she saw in their eyes hurt her. Donna was under no illusions about the way she looked. Women were always hunting for the perfect body while she was happy with her size sixteen curves. There were few pleasures in this world, and she still loved eating. Her mother and her foster mother had been fantastic cooks, and she'd never been one to turn down something amazing. She'd taken after their skill into the kitchen herself, and she loved to cook.

"I don't date because men want the ideal model on the cover of a magazine."

"I'm not like most men." He took her hand, turning her palm over in his. She liked his touch way too much. Caleb stroked along her inner wrist. "And I think it's time you stopped treating me like other men."

She couldn't think with his hands on her. He caressed over her pulse. Staring down at his large hands, she actually looked delicate in comparison. Licking her lips, she forced herself to look into his black eyes.

"I'm here. You can't keep pestering me at work."

"Baby, I'm not going to stop pestering you until I get what I want."

"And what do you want?" She was almost afraid to ask what he wanted.

"Don't you know?" he asked, smiling. His smile was like that of a wolf before he was about to get his prey.

Donna didn't say another word. She stared at Caleb waiting. He continued to rub her wrist as he spoke.

"I want to fuck you, Donna."

His words sent a thrill down her spine even as she was embarrassed by his bluntness.

Averting her eyes, she glanced down at the dance floor to see Lydia with her boyfriend, dancing. They were both having a good time as they were wrapped around each other. Did she want that?

"This is not good." She tried to pull her hand away, but he wouldn't release her.

"You're not going anywhere yet. You promised me tonight, and I intend to collect. Look at me."

She turned to stare at him, gritting her teeth as something tugged deep inside her. "What?" she asked.

"You're going to back out of tonight?"

"You blackmailed me into it."

Caleb smiled. "Relax, Donna. We're getting to know each other. I'll take you out to the dance floor, and we can dance and have a little fun." He leaned back and stared at her.

Sitting back, she watched as a waitress approached them placing their drinks on the table. Caleb thanked the woman without taking his gaze away from her.

"So, you own this nightclub?" she asked.

"Yes. I'm a joint owner with a friend and partner."

"It seems nice." Biting her lip, she looked down at her lap wondering what the hell she was supposed to talk about.

He reached out to grab his drink, and she noticed his knuckles.

"Owning this place, is that all you do?" she asked.

Caleb stared at her, his dark eyes stripping away years of protection to see deep inside her soul.

Shaking her head, she did her best to push the thoughts out of her mind.

"Yes, why wouldn't it?" he asked.

"Bruised knuckles and the suit, they don't match." She tapped her leg, looking around the VIP section. Donna didn't recognize anyone. If they were superstars she didn't notice them or know where they were from.

"Some customers do not take no for an answer. I help where I can."

She frowned. "Since when did a businessman do his own dirty work?"

"This one does and has since he learned it was better to do things this way rather than relying on someone else." He lifted his leg over his knee and rested his head in his hand, staring at her. "Now, I've got questions."

She tensed, waiting.

"Why don't you have a boyfriend?" he asked.

Letting out a sigh, she pushed some hair out of her face. "I don't want one."

"Sex?"

"We don't know each other that well. I'm not going to tell you what I do."

His gaze didn't waver.

"You've never had sex or been with a man," he said.

She felt her cheeks heat even as she fought the embarrassment threatening to claim her.

"I'm not going anywhere no matter how much you ignore me."

"Have you had sex?" she asked.

"Yes."

"With another man?" She fired the question at him trying to make him feel like he was her.

Caleb chuckled. "No. I've not fucked a man. I've screwed a whole list of women. I've lost count of the number of women I've been with."

Jealousy struck her hard, surprising her. She didn't know what to expect from him and certainly didn't see him as boyfriend material. Donna wasn't stupid. She knew what sex involved and how it happened.

Stumbling around the internet she'd found plenty of porn readily available.

"So you've been with a lot of women. The bracelet you bought the other day, was that for a woman?"

"Yes. It was a parting gift."

"You give a gift to dump the woman?"

He nodded. "I want to take you to my bed, strip you naked, and fuck you."

She paused in reaching out for her soda and glanced at him.

"You should know I'm not going to let you go until I get what I want."

"I'm not going to sleep with you," Donna said.

"Baby, when I get you to my bed, we're not going to be doing any sleeping. I'm going to have you screaming in pleasure."

Caleb handed her the soda that she'd pulled away from.

She took the glass from his hands and took a sip. In all of her life she'd never been bombarded with such masculinity. Caleb was filled with it, oozing out of every pore.

He removed his jacket and rolled up the sleeves of his shirt. The ink on his arms took her by surprise. She glanced over the dance floor in time to see Lydia leaving the floor. Her friend approached the bar, and one of the guards pointed up to the VIP section.

"I'm not ready to be interrupted." Caleb took the soda from her hands and lifted her to her feet.

"What are you doing?" she asked.

"We're going to dance." Before she could say anything more, they were heading down to the dance floor. Lydia and Darren passed them.

"Where are you going?" Lydia asked.

"Dancing." Caleb answered for her, tugging her onto the floor. She didn't get a chance to say anything else as he took the lead.

People on the floor made a space for him. He spun her around and pulled her close. Caleb's hand landed on the base of her back. His body was flush against hers. She felt each line, and he held her close, making it hard for her to get away.

"You were rude."

"I didn't want to be interrupted. Your friend has an opinion, and I'm not interested in what she's got to say." His fingers caressed her through the dress, making it hard for her to think.

"Lydia's a friend. She worries about me."

"And she annoys me. If I wanted to know what she had to say, I'd have given her my time." The music faded into the background along with all the people. At first she noticed all the women eyeing up Caleb. Then she just stopped thinking about them as his gaze trapped her.

"Do you like your job?" he asked.

She shrugged. "It pays the bills, and it beats doing anything else."

"Why don't you let anyone get close to you?"

"Why are you asking so many questions?"

"I'm interested about you."

Glancing at his chest, she tried to get her thoughts into focus. Nothing was making any sense to her.

"You must be confusing me with someone else."

How did a man who owned a nightclub get bruises that were clearly from a fight? What was he hiding that he didn't want her to know?

"You're thinking too hard." He pressed a thumb between her brows. "Stop thinking and allow your body to feel."

She didn't trust her body. Her mind was much more reliable than anything else. Caleb was not all what he seemed. Donna knew he was going to hurt her heart if she let him, and the only way to stay in control was to try to push him away.

Chapter Four

Donna's body was soft against his. Caleb ran his fingers up and down her spine, going a little lower each time. She rested her head against his chest, and he closed his eyes for the briefest of seconds to simply enjoy the feel of her. Never in all of his life had he enjoyed a woman being so close to him.

Her friends were far away. From the look in Lydia's eyes, Caleb knew she was going to cause them trouble. He had files on both of Lydia and Darren. Getting what he wanted required information. He knew the only way to get Donna was to find her friends' weaknesses. Lydia had a lot of debt from a previous relationship. She ran up credit card bills along with a few medical bills.

Darren wasn't much of a concern. He was Lydia's latest beau and didn't show any signs of wanting to be anything more.

The song moved into another more upbeat one. Caleb didn't stop holding her close even as others looked his way annoyed. He shot them a glare. Most of the people in the club knew who he was.

"You've got to give me a chance," he said.

She looked up toward him. Once again he was blown away by the intensity of her blue eyes.

"Why?"

"Haven't you ever just wanted to do something crazy that was against all of your other plans?" he asked.

Donna bit her lip but didn't look away.

"Give me a chance to be more."

"I don't know what you're talking about. You asked for a date to leave me alone. What more do you want?"

"I want the chance to do this." He stroked her cheek with the backs of his fingers then tilted her head back. Dropping his head down, he covered her lips with his own. He didn't give her time to think as he ran his tongue along the seam of her lips.

She moaned. The sound vibrated through her body. Wrapping both arms around her, he cupped her full, round ass and drew her close. Rubbing his rock hard cock against her front, he felt her squirm in his arms. He didn't want the contact to end. Donna opened her lips on a gasp, and he plundered her mouth, tasting her.

Deepening the kiss, he refused to release her. He wanted her naked, open and ready to take his cock.

"Boss," Henry said, interrupting the moment.

Pulling away, he kept hold of her as he turned to look at his friend.

"What?" he asked.

"We've got a few problems in the back." Henry raised a brow, waiting.

"I'm coming." Taking hold of Donna's hand he walked her back to the VIP section. Lydia was frowning at him as he placed Donna back in her seat. "Please feel free to drink and dance to your heart's content." Turning his attention to his woman, he focused on her. "Don't leave until we finish our discussion."

"There was nothing to discuss."

"There was plenty to discuss. Don't leave."

He waited for her to nod then followed Henry back down to the main floor. The brothel part of the club was located on the back side of the building near the warehouses. Men who were willing to pay knew how to get access.

"You're making a mistake with her," Henry said.

"I told you that you were making a mistake fucking endless whores, but you still did it and you got an

41

infection." Caleb rolled down his sleeves covering up his ink. He'd forgotten about his ink while in Donna's company. She'd not even taken the time to look at them.

"There's a difference."

"What?" Caleb asked, pressing the button of the elevator toward the top floor.

"I'm not at risk of falling in love with the whores I'm with. You are."

"Your point?"

"Donna Smith is not a whore. You'd have to be blind not to see the difference between her and all the other women you've been with. Donna's a kitten in comparison to the lionesses you've been with."

Caleb chuckled at Henry's comparison. "I like her."

"In our business it's dangerous to like and fall in love. We're strong, Caleb. We keep our shit together, but we still have weaknesses. There are men out there who would do anything to get our club, our girls, and our trade. I'm not willing to risk our livelihood for a woman you know nothing about."

"I know her."

"No, you don't. She's a woman, Caleb."

"I'm not in love with her, Henry. I'm only interested in fucking her, and I'd rather not hear about how much you're worried. I've never let a pussy rule my decision. I'm not about to start now, not even for Donna." Caleb was intrigued by the blonde beauty, nothing more.

He wanted to know if her cunt was as tight as he imagined. Her tits reeled him in, and all he could imagine doing was sucking and fucking them. There was more to her than he wanted to believe.

"Yeah, keep telling yourself that," Henry said.

The scent of cheap perfume overwhelmed Caleb as he entered the brothel part of their business. He tried to keep this as much a secret as possible. It helped to have a couple of men who were members of the police force who liked to get their rocks off. Caleb wasn't picky. He'd blackmailed plenty of the cops to keep them off his back. Some men couldn't be bought no matter how much he wanted to. Women walked past him in different stages of undress. They tried to capture his attention, but he wasn't interested.

He heard the yelling before he even got there.

Tensing up he rounded the corner and found what he was looking for. A man in his late twenties or early thirties was throwing shit around and yelling. Caleb saw the whore on the ground cupping her nose. Blood poured from the wound, and he was pissed off.

"What the fuck is going on here?"

The man rounded on him. "That fucking bitch wouldn't give me what I fucking paid for." Spittle flew out of the man's mouth. Taking his time, Caleb looked around the man and glanced at the girl on the floor.

"What did he want?"

"I wanted fucking anal!"

The girl cried out as the customer grabbed her arm and hauled her up. Caleb lost his temper. Landing the blow to the man's mouth, he shoved him making sure the other man wasn't holding onto the girl.

Henry took hold of the girl as Caleb had the man trapped against the wall.

"I was letting him have what he wanted, but he didn't want to use a rubber or lube. I'm not going to do anal without a rubber and lube." The girl was sobbing. Caleb recognized her as Roxie, one of his good workers.

"We've got rules here, fucker."

"It's a whorehouse. There are no rules. These bitches fuck for money. I can get better service on the fucking streets."

Caleb smiled. "Then go out to the streets."

"I want my money."

"You damaged one of my girls. Henry, get me a knife." Caleb didn't let the man go.

"What the fuck you going to do? Is this to scare me?"

Laughing, Caleb shook his head. "No, it's not to scare you. It's to send a message."

"What message?"

The knife landed in his hand. Staring at the man in front of him, Caleb felt a sense of peace as he looked at the bastard who'd scared one of the women he'd sworn to protect.

Sliding the blade across his face, Caleb struck. "No man touches one of my girls and gets away with it."

He worked the blade from the man's cheek, up his head then across. The screams from the women could be heard in the background as he went to work. After he was finished with the knife, he dropped the blade and slammed his fist into the guy's ribs. Over and over, Caleb stuck to his reputation of being a hard assed man. He wasn't going to let anyone think they could poach on his territory. The girls in Ecstasy were his, and no one got a chance to touch or look at them without abiding by the rules. These girls were all his, and he'd protect them for as long as they needed it. Henry didn't stop him.

When his message had gotten across, he turned toward his man. "Get rid of the body and make sure those bitches know to keep their fucking mouths shut." His hands were shaking, and he was covered in blood from the sudden attack.

"They know not to say anything," Henry said.

"Why didn't you take care of this?" Caleb unbuttoned his shirt. Blood stained the cuffs and the main breast of his shirt.

"To remind you of who you are."

He paused and looked at his friend. "What?"

"You're forgetting where you come from. We're not the kind of men to make a joke out of something like this. Donna, she seems like a nice woman, but we're not nice men. Think about that before you allow yourself the chance to be with her."

"I'll fuck whoever I want."

"When it interferes with our job, it becomes my business." Henry moved toward one of the wardrobes and pulled out a shirt. "Put this on."

Caleb knew he wasn't going to end it. At least, he wasn't going to end it until he'd gotten a taste of her.

****

Taking a sip of her drink, Donna glanced around the club enjoying the beat of the music as it pulsed. The energy in the air was addictive, and she loved watching people dance. She'd enjoyed being in Caleb's arms a lot more than she liked. He knew how to hold her and to lead her into a dance that made her not want to stop. She'd been disappointed when he brought her to her seat.

"Donna, do you know what you're doing?" Lydia asked.

Donna looked toward her friend, seeing the worry on her face. "It's just a date."

"No, it's more than that. You didn't see the way you two were dancing."

"Lydia, stop," Darren said. "You don't have to talk about this."

Donna glanced toward Darren seeing the concern of his face.

"No, I will talk about it. She's never been on a single date, and all of a sudden this guy comes out of nowhere and pretty much tells her to date him. He's creepy, and I don't agree with it."

"It's okay, Lydia. You said I should go out dating more."

"Grow the fuck up, Donna. He's forcing you to be here."

She stared down at her lap and wished her friend wouldn't make any more of a scene.

"Donna," Caleb said, drawing all of their attention back to him.

Jerking in her seat, she turned to see him standing, in a different shirt, staring at her. The shirt he'd worn before had white buttons whereas the one he was wearing now had black buttons and looked wrinkled.

"Hey."

"Would you like to go home?" he asked.

She looked back to her friends. Darren was whispering in Lydia's ear.

The last conversation hadn't made her want to stay in the club.

"Yes, if you don't mind." She put her soda down on the table and smiled at her friend. "I'll see you at work tomorrow."

"Look, I'm sorry."

Holding her hand up, Donna tried to push her concern away.

"Don't worry about it. I know you care." She leaned down to hug her friend before standing up. "Take care of her."

Darren nodded.

Taking hold of Caleb's hand, she followed him down to the main part of the club and then through the exit.

"Your friend's wrong."

She turned toward Caleb. "What happened to your shirt?"

He tensed up. It was only the slightest of movements that she detected, but it was there.

"Business."

A car was waiting beside the road. Caleb helped her into the passenger side before he climbed into the driver's side.

"Lydia means well."

"Your friend needs to learn not to stick her nose where it doesn't belong." He put the car into gear.

Donna decided to stay quiet as he'd gotten snappy with her within minutes of being back in his company. She stared out of the window knowing any kind of future with him was going to be a mistake.

"You can talk to me," he said.

Turning to look at him, she shook her head. "I'm good. I'm happy just to go home." She frowned when she realized she'd not told him where she lived, yet he was driving in the right direction. "I've not given you my home address."

"I know what I need to know."

"How?"

"I just do."

Lydia was right. Donna didn't know anything about this guy, and he'd invaded her life.

"After you drop me off home I don't want to see you again."

"You don't mean that."

"I do." She wasn't into being yelled out or snapped at by a guy she barely knew. Caleb was new to her. She hadn't known him longer than a week, and the time they'd spent together could be easily rounded up to a couple of hours.

"Fuck!" He slammed his palm against the wheel of the car.

She cried out as the car swerved nearly hitting another vehicle coming toward them.

"Will you stop? You're going to get us both killed."

"I can take care of a fucking car."

"You're a jerk."

Tightening her hands into fists, she tried her best to get her emotions in check. Her heart was racing.

Caleb pulled up outside of her apartment block. Without waiting for him, she opened the door and ran toward the door. He was on her within seconds.

"Donna, stop."

"No, you're insane, crazy even."

Grabbing her key from inside her purse, she didn't look behind her as she ran for her front door. He continued to call her.

Opening her door she was about to slam it closed when he stopped her with a palm on her door.

"Leave me alone," she said.

"Let me in. I don't want to leave shit like this."

"You've got bad manners. You're rude and unfair. I've done nothing wrong, and yet you were treating me like crap. I'm not letting you inside my apartment. I'm not letting you near me."

His gaze darkened, became lethal almost.

Caleb showed her that he could do whatever the hell he wanted. He shoved the door, and she stepped out of the way, dropping her bag and keys in the process.

In one motion he had the door closed and was standing within her apartment glaring at her.

She was alone with no one else to save her.

Her heart raced, and she watched as he ran fingers through his hair.

"You're scared?"

"You've just forced your way into my apartment. Of course I'm scared." She took a step back and paused as he followed her.

"I'm not going to hurt you."

"No? I doubt it. I don't know anything about you." She held her hand up in front as if to ward him of.

He took a step closer.

"You've got bloody knuckles. I know the only way to get them is a fight. You've hit someone recently. I don't want to get in the way of whatever your problem is." She was shaking.

Caleb stood inside her apartment, and Pearl was nowhere to be found. Her cat was probably hiding in her wardrobe or sleeping.

"I'm not going to hurt you, but I'm not going to accept the fact you're not going to see me again."

"I don't want to see you. You promised if I came to the club, which I did, you'd leave me alone. I did my part, and I'm asking you to leave."

For several seconds he simply stared at her without talking.

"Fine, you want me to leave then I'll leave, but first I want something from you."

"What?" Part of her was disappointed that he was just going to leave. He scared her and excited her at the same time. Not once had she felt this alive, this exhilarated.

You're a freak.

He took a step closer, and she took a step away.

"Stop moving away."

"Tell me what you want and I'll stop."

"It doesn't work like that, pet."

She forced herself to stop and stare at him. "What do you want?" Fisting her palms at her side, she waited for him to make the first move.

He closed the distance between them.

Caleb reached out, sinking his fingers into her hair. "You're incredibly beautiful. Do you know that?"

She shook her head.

"From the first moment I looked at you, I knew I wanted you. Then I looked into your eyes and saw something, I don't fucking know what I saw. I'm not going to let this go, and after this, you can tell me to leave."

His lips crushed against hers stopping all kind of thought from her mind. She gripped his shoulders and moaned as he plundered her mouth with his tongue. His other hand cupped her ass drawing her closer.

She felt the hard length of his cock pressing against her stomach.

"You feel that, Donna. That's what you do to me. When we were looking at bracelets for the whore I was fucking, I was thinking about you. I wanted to spread you out and look at that virginal pussy. You are a virgin, aren't you, baby?"

Donna whimpered.

He claimed her mouth as his hand went back up her body and around to cup her breast.

She gasped as he pinched her nipple.

"You're into this as much as I am." He walked her back until the wall stopped them. Caleb pushed her shirt down revealing her bra-covered breast. He pushed the bra out of the way until her breast was naked for him to touch and see.

"What are you doing?" she asked.

"Tell me to stop."

Gritting her teeth, she shook her head. Heat gathered in her pussy as he thumbed her nipple.

"Then I'm going to play." He kissed down to her neck, sucking on her pulse.

She couldn't focus on any one sensation as he sucked at her neck then touched her breast.

He went down until he sucked her nipple into his mouth. Crying out, she arched up against him needing more of what he could offer.

Glancing down she saw him circle her nipple then suck her breast into his mouth. His other hand left her hair, sliding down her body.

You need to stop this.

Donna knew what she should do, but she liked his touch way too much. His fingers slid up the inside of her thigh then landed over her pussy.

Crying out, she closed her eyes, opening her legs wider.

"You're so fucking wet, baby. Are you sure you want me to leave?"

She shook her head. "No, I don't want you to leave."

The words broke from her lips even though she didn't want to say them.

He pushed her panties out of the way, and he stroked a finger down her slit. Opening her eyes, she stared down. Caleb had her dress down to her waist and bunched up around his hand. She looked wanton, completely unlike her.

His fingers pressed against her clit, pushing her closer to orgasm.

"You're going to come against my fingers, Donna. Give me that sweet cum."

She shook her head, denying him.

Caleb released her breasts and slammed his tongue into her mouth. She kissed him back, needing him to finish what he started. He nibbled on her lip then went back to sucking on her nipples.

There was nothing else she could do to stop what he'd started. Screaming out her release, she held onto him throughout. He kept her upright against the wall after each shudder of her orgasm.

When it was over, she watched him suck the fingers that were on her pussy into his mouth. The scent of her arousal floated between them. His digits were slick with her release.

"You taste as sweet as I imagined."

"Caleb?"

He silenced her with another kiss.

"I don't want to hear another word from you. If you don't want to feel that again I understand." She wanted to tell him to shut up. "But if you want to feel like that and better then meet me at the corner café Sunday morning. You're not at work then, and we'll see where this goes."

With one final kiss he left her apartment, closing the door behind him.

Chapter Five

Caleb closed his cell phone and ordered another coffee from the waitress as he stared out of the café windows. He had a full view of who was coming and going, just the way he liked it. Henry was nowhere in sight. He'd told his friend not to bother coming. Since the problem of Friday, he'd not spoken a word of Donna to his partner. He wasn't afraid of being with Donna.

She was the complete opposite of him, sweet to his mean, nice to his cruel. Thinking about her over the last day he'd gotten hard imagining her partially naked up against the wall. He could have taken her there and then. She wouldn't have the time to tell him no, but he'd stopped. For once in his life, Caleb had decided to be the better man.

He had blood on his hands, a lot of blood. In his fighting days he'd killed men for fun, and now he killed men to send a message. Drugs, women, all of that was all on him, and no one was ever going to change him, not even Donna. Henry's fear was misguided.

Running a finger along his lip, he recalled the sweet taste of her cunt. He'd never tasted a woman in his life. The women he fucked were not the kind he wanted to taste with his mouth.

Would she be brave enough to come to him today?

The anticipation was driving him insane. He'd wait all day if he had to just to get what he wanted.

He didn't know what would come after he fucked her. Most of the time, he lost all interest in the women he fucked after he'd taken them.

"Can I help you, sir?" the waitress asked, smiling at him. Her chest was thrust out, inviting him in.

"No!"

Drumming his fingers on the table he waited for the woman he really wanted. She had to come. The disappointment he saw in Donna's eyes when he'd walked away told him he was making the right choice.

Donna needed to come to him before he went back to her. She'd been scared of him, terrified, yet she'd wanted him. Her cunt had been soaking wet, begging for his cock.

One taste of her might not even be enough for him.

Taking a sip of his coffee, he looked up as the doorbell chimed.

Donna stood there, looking as nervous as she had the night before last. When she saw him, her cheeks went a beautiful shade of red.

Come on, baby, be strong.

Bowing her head, she walked toward him, pulling out a seat and sitting down. She removed her jacket to reveal a simple white shirt over her jeans. She clasped her hands together and looked at him. "I'm here."

"You're here." He took a longer sip of his coffee, looking at her over the rim of his glass.

"You didn't give me a time, and I didn't know if I was going to turn up." She licked her lips, glancing left and right.

He signaled to the waitress, who came immediately.

His cock hardened at the sight of Donna. Part of him couldn't believe she'd come, but then another part knew how he was going to spend the day with her. This was not going to be a long courtship. The curiosity in her eyes told him that.

When a coffee was placed in front of her, he leaned on the table.

"You turned up. So what does that mean?"

"I don't know." She shrugged, lifting her cup to her lips. "I was hoping you'd tell me."

Caleb smiled. "Well, we can either take this slowly or we can go fast."

"What do you mean?"

"You liked what I did to you?" he asked.

"Yes."

"Do you want to feel that way again?"

She tucked some hair behind her ear. "Yes." Her word was a small whisper.

"I didn't hear you. You're going to have to speak up."

"Yes, I want more of what you did Friday night."

"I'm not a forever kind of guy. If we're doing this then we're doing it my way." He reached over taking her hand. "I'm never going to love you. Don't expect me to love you or to settle down with kids. I also expect you to get on birth control. I'll wear a rubber the first couple of times, but then I'm going to expect you to take care of protection." She opened her mouth to speak, but he continued on before giving her chance to speak. "There will be no other men for you. We do this then you're mine, and I won't allow scraps that other men leave behind."

She opened her mouth and then closed her lips. "This was in fact a mistake."

He held her hand as she made to get up. "You're not leaving."

"Yes, I am. You're a pig. A sexist, horrid pig. I can't believe I was looking forward to seeing you again. You're horrid and disgusting."

"But you came because you wanted me."

"No, I wanted the man who was with me Friday night, not this. First, you can wear a rubber. I've tried birth control, and it messed with my body. I was sick, and

I can't be on it. Second, how dare you tell me this when you've slept with no end of women? I've never been with anyone, and yet you want me to allow your diseased penis inside *my* body? You've got to be kidding me." She tugged out of his hold and stood. "This was a mistake." He watched as she threw a bill down on the table. "Forget I ever came here."

He should just let her walk out of the café, but he couldn't. Throwing more bills onto the table, he rushed out to follow her. She was heading in the direction of her apartment. Grabbing her arm, he pulled her down an alleyway that was clear.

"Fine, I'll wear the fucking rubbers," he said, pressing her against the wall.

"This isn't just about the rubbers. You're being a jerk, and I'm not signing on with anyone or anything when they're being jerks and vile." She spat the words at him, and for the first time since he'd seen her, Caleb witnessed the fire inside her. Her eyes sparked anger, glinting in the shade.

His cock awakened to that fire, and he knew he couldn't let her go before he had a taste. She'd drive him crazy. Henry was right. She was different, but even as he thought all of this, he couldn't help but need more.

"Then I stop being a jerk to you."

"You can't just stop."

"Yes, I can. I can be whatever you need me to be." He pressed his lips to hers, running his tongue along her lip. "I'm not giving up."

"No, you've got to stop."

"Are you not hot for me right now? Is your pussy dry or wet for me?"

She shook her head. "Stop this, Caleb."

"I'm not stopping anything. I get what I want." He pulled back seeing the fight still in her eyes. "I won't be a jerk. I'm used to dealing with women like this. I don't offer them anything else."

"Then forget about them. I'm not most women, and I refuse to be treated like that." There were tears in her eyes.

"Are you coming with me?"

Donna stayed silent. She pressed her lips together, closing her eyes. "I don't think I should."

"Don't think, baby. Let your body do all the talking for you." He pressed his cock against her stomach. "This is what's driving me, Donna. This is how you make me feel. I don't want to give this up. I need you, baby."

"You're confusing me."

"And you're driving me crazy." Never, not once, not even in the ring, had he begged a person for something. He was more than willing to beg now to get what he wanted, what he needed.

"Okay." She spoke after some time had passed. He didn't know how much, only that he was desperate to hear her voice speaking the words he wanted to hear. "I'll come with you back to your place, but you've got to promise to let me go when I'm ready."

He nodded. There was no chance of him letting her go. Caleb knew what he wanted.

"Come on. My car's parked a few blocks from here." He took her hand, feeling the shake within her fingers.

Was she still scared of him?

Donna remained silent as she walked beside him. They passed many people on their way to his car. He didn't give them a passing thought. Moving quickly, Caleb didn't want her to change her mind. This was happening now, and the excitement was pulsing within his veins to get her alone.

Pulling out his keys, he beeped the car, and helped her into the passenger side of his vehicle. Locking her inside with the child lock, he circled the vehicle to his own side.

Without saying a word, he pulled out of the parking lot and headed into the center of the city. He wasn't going to take her back to the club where there was a risk of other people invading their space. The brothel never closed, and he'd been with women who walked in and out of the apartment. He did allow it but not with Donna. She was different.

Glancing toward her, he saw her hands were clenched into tight fists that were leaving her knuckles white.

Putting his foot firmly on the accelerator, he tried to get to his place as fast as he could.

****

What the hell are you doing, Donna?

Closing her eyes, she tried to think of all the logical reasons as to why she shouldn't be sat in this car with a man she barely knew. All of her old teachings of getting into cars with strange men came rushing back to her. She shouldn't be there, but yet, the tingling along her lips left her wanting more.

Caleb made her want things she didn't think she'd ever want. It was all insane, exciting, and she couldn't stop herself from wanting more.

"You don't have to be afraid. I won't hurt you."

Wouldn't he? During their last couple of conversations he'd said stuff that hurt her. He was gruff, crude, and rude. She didn't like him, and yet her body was alight whenever she was around him. The city went by, and she was aware of the closeness the car provided them. He could reach out and touch her. She craved his touch as much as she craved her next breath.

What's wrong with you?

He turned off to the right and followed the road down to an underground parking facility.

"Where are we?" she asked.

"We're at my apartment. Henry's got a place a couple of floor down. I'm on the twelfth floor." She saw a signpost next to one of the parking spaces with Caleb's name.

"Does owning your own club make good money?" She slapped her palm against her mouth. "I'm so sorry. I can't believe I asked that."

He chuckled. "I make enough."

She noticed he didn't actually answer the question. Staring at him, she waited to see if he'd add more. He didn't.

Caleb parked the car and opened his door. He didn't give her chance to back out. She followed him outside, and he was beside her door within moments, slamming the door closed. Taking the hand he offered, she moved behind him toward the elevator. Not once did he speak, leaving the silence to stretch between them.

Do you know what you're doing?

No.

Does Lydia at least know where you are?

No.

He could kill you and no one would know or care.

Gritting her teeth, she tried to fight the fear suddenly gripping her.

The elevator pinged open. This was her last chance to leave without fear. Glancing at Caleb, she stopped. There was no way she could leave. She wanted to know where this would go a lot more than she wanted to leave.

She took one step in front of the other, following him down the long corridor. He didn't release her hand even as he grabbed the key from his pocket and opened the door.

This was entirely on her if she passed over the threshold. Licking her lips, she stepped over the line, and Caleb followed. He closed the door, and they were entirely alone. No one would interrupt them. They only had each other for company.

"Give me your jacket."

Turning her back to him, she removed her outer jacket and gripped her purse tightly. She wasn't scared of him stealing from her. Keeping a firm hand on her purse meant she was able to ground herself. It was strange, but holding her purse stopped her from doing anything stupid.

He took hold of her purse. "Let's put that down, baby." He took her last security blanket with him.

You can do this.

Caleb turned back to her, reaching out to grab her arms. He walked her back, and she couldn't tear her gaze away from his. His eyes were so dark they were almost black, and his touch was firm, not painful.

Her heart raced as the noises around them faded into nothing.

He moved her into the main sitting room. There was no coffee table to stop their movements.

"Stop panicking."

"I'm not."

He cupped her cheek, tilting her head back with his thumbs underneath her chin.

"Your skin is so smooth and flawless." He stroked her cheek with the back of his fingers before returning to hold her head at a particular angle.

Her mouth dried up as his head got closer. His lips brushed across hers, lighting a fire she didn't think was ever going to be put out.

He slid his tongue along her bottom lip, gliding around then pressing inside. She opened her mouth accepting him inside her lips. Closing her eyes, she melted against him the moment he touched her. His left hand left her face to move down her body. The backs of his fingers grazed her breast. He went down until he held the bottom of her shirt.

Jerking back, she looked him in the eye.

"I want to see you, Donna."

She didn't stop him, nor did she help him to remove her clothing. He tugged the shirt up her body then over her head. Instinctively, she covered her breasts wanting to hide herself from him.

He wouldn't let her hide away from his touch. "Don't ever cover yourself from me. I want to see what belongs to me."

Donna couldn't dispute him. He gripped her wrists and forced her hands away from her body. Taking in several deep breaths, she waited for him to finish what he started. Caleb didn't rush to do what he wanted. He took his time staring at her. She wore a simple white lace bra and a pair of panties to match, but he hadn't seen them yet.

"They're so sweet, and modest."

Her cheeks heated under his gaze.

"On you, it looks beautiful."

"Haven't you ever seen a woman with white underwear?"

"No. I haven't." His dark gaze returned to her. "This is all new to me, baby. I'm used to whores and women who don't want fuck all from me but a nice stiff cock and some money."

She jerked back but stopped herself from covering her body.

Caleb reached for the buttons on his shirt and started to reveal the expanse of his chest and the ink all over him. He tore the shirt from his chest, and she saw the array of ink. His body was like a canvas for a tattoo parlor. The ink on his arms caught her attention first. Down his left arm she noticed the cross, and below it was a graveyard, each tattoo so intricately designed to the point she could see the strips of wood.

"You like to get inked."

"I like a hell of a lot more, baby." He lifted his arm up and ran fingers through his hair. His left arm had two pictures of the same symbol, the devil. One devil was in the male form while the other in a female form.

His chest and abs had small designs that were not related to any other.

He stepped closer wrapping his arms around her body.

"You've got to leave those inhibitions out the door. I'm not your judge, juror, or executioner. I've done shit I'm not proud of, Donna. I'm here because I want you. Do the same."

With one quick move he released her bra and pulled the straps down her arms. The cool air stroked across her breasts. Staring into his eyes, she forced all of her inhibitions out of her body, trying to focus on their here and now. Nothing else mattered in her life. The only person who cared about her was her work colleague, Lydia. Her cat Pearl meant something to her. Both her family and foster family were dead. The only person she could rely upon was herself.

The bra dropped to the floor. His hands captured her breasts, pushing them together and thumbing both her nipples. Crying out, she flung her head back at the pleasure he created by touching her.

"That's right, Donna. Know who's here wanting you."

Gripping her arms, she watched him touching her. His large hands with the bruised knuckles touched her with a tenderness she didn't expect from him.

"Don't hurt me," she said.

"I won't." He leaned down and took one of her nipples into his mouth. The pleasure went from her breast straight to her core. There was no room for anything else. She closed her eyes, wincing a little at the sudden pain. He sucked, tonguing the bead, then slid across to take the other breast into his mouth.

Biting her lip she tried to keep her cries inside.

"Don't hide them from me. I want to hear everything you've got to say and scream," he said.

Whimpering, she shook her head.

"You don't give me everything I want, then I stop this here and now."

She opened her mouth and released the cries he wished to hear. There was no holding back. Sinking her fingers into his hair, she held him against her, loving the way he tongued her nipples.

"Caleb." She moaned his name as he moved from one breast to the other. He fingered the button of her jeans, and before she could stop him, he opened the denim and pushed it down her thighs. She kicked off her sneakers and helped him push the fabric down.

He stepped away from her, tugging off his own jeans in the process. His cock was covered by a pair of briefs. The outline of his cock was clear to see. Caleb was long and thick.

Glancing back up at him, he wrapped his arm around her. "It's time to take this out of the bedroom."

She didn't fight him as he moved her back a little more. "I can walk where you need me."

"I know. I like the way you feel against me. I'm not going to give that up." She gasped as he slapped her ass. The rough slap sent another shockwave of pleasure rushing through her. "You like a little pain?"

Donna shook her head. She didn't have a clue what she liked. She was in no doubt as to what Caleb had in store for her by the end of the day.

Chapter Six

Caleb left the bedroom door open. In all of his years of fucking women, he'd never taken the time to consider a woman's needs. All the time, in the past that he'd been with a woman, he didn't care if she was wet or into it. Lube helped that problem, and he was happy to use it with the women. With Donna, he wanted her slick because of him. The white underwear undid him. His arousal was on the verge of pain, yet he wasn't begging to slam her to the ground and fuck her until she couldn't think.

Instead, he was taking his time with his little virgin.

Her tits were large and her nipples small. He was used to his women being on the slender side, but her larger size didn't turn him away from her. There was no way he was going to be turned away from her. She was beautiful, sweet, and inviting.

Cupping her head, he claimed her lips, sliding his tongue into her mouth, thinking about his dick being inside her sweet cunt.

"That's right, baby, open up for me."

She responded to each touch and caress he gave her. Donna opened her mouth to his tongue and met him halfway. Running his hands down her body, he pressed against her nipples then caressed down to her panties. In one tug, he tore them from her body. She squealed and jerked back. "You've ruined my underwear."

"I don't like underwear. Its only function is to get in my way. I don't want it in my way anymore." He chuckled and pressed her down to the bed.

"What are you doing?"

"I'm going to make you feel good." He went down to his knees, gripped her fleshy thighs, and spread her open. Fine hairs dusted her mound. "Lie back."

She hesitated for a second before doing as he instructed and lay back. He stared at her pretty pink pussy. Her clit was swollen, peeking out from behind the hood. He stared at her entrance, knowing he was going to be inside her within minutes.

The musky scent of her arousal wafted up to his nose. He never gave oral to other women, but with Donna, he wanted to. There was so much he wanted to do, craved to do, with her. His mouth watered for a small taste. Opening the lips of her sex with his fingers, he licked along her slit. He went to the opening of her pussy then up to circle her clit. Over and over he did this, and her taste exploded on his tongue.

He lapped at her cunt, licking her juices. Donna screamed and cried out above him, begging him to stop then begging for more. He didn't stop and loved every second of the sounds she made. Scoring his teeth over her nub, he flicked his tongue over and around seeing what actions set her off more than others. Out of the corner of his eye he saw her gripping the edge of the sheet.

Her hand was in a tight fist in the blanket.

When he couldn't wait any longer, he focused on her nub, and he was rewarded as Donna shattered into climax. Nudging her up the bed, he removed the boxer briefs that kept him contained. Fisting his shaft, he stared down at her soft body, knowing he couldn't miss the opportunity to claim her without a condom. He was going straight to hell anyway.

Caleb knew the risks of what he was about to do, but he couldn't stop it. Climbing up the bed, he slid his naked dick through her creamy slit. She was soaking wet and open. Coating his tip in her cum, he aligned the tip to her entrance.

She whispered his name.

Ignoring her call, he watched his cock as with one smooth thrust he slammed inside her to the hilt. Her tight heat surrounded him, gripping tighter than any vise.

"Stop!" She screamed for him to stop. He caught hold of her hands and held them beside her head. Resting his head against hers, he tried to gain control of his wayward body. Nothing could stop him from taking her. "Please, you're hurting me."

He silenced her with his lips. "You're a virgin. It will hurt the first time. Give it a moment and it will get better." Caleb hoped it got better. He wasn't a rapist, but he didn't know if he'd be able to stop.

Closing his eyes, he tried to think of anything but the clenching of her cunt wrapped around his cock.

Count sheep.

Don't count sheep, fuck her pussy. She wants it. She needs it.

Locking his fingers with hers, he took deep breaths waiting for her to stop squirming.

"Stop moving before I lose all chance of being nice, Donna."

"You promised not to hurt me."

"You're a virgin. There's going to be some pain." *I've also forgotten the condom on purpose. I could knock you up.* He kept the latter to himself not wanting to deal with her upset.

Her tight cunt was wet and perfect.

He couldn't give this up easily. She was untouched, and he was the first man to take her. The knowledge of being her first, knowing his cock was the only one to have been inside her, sent something primitive off in his mind. No other man knew Donna's sweetness. She was perfect, sweet, and totally his.

If he knocked her up, she couldn't get rid of him.

Caleb tried to force the plan out of his mind. There was no way he could get her pregnant and hope she accepted it.

Kissing her lips, he nibbled her bottom lip hoping to get her to open up.

"Relax, baby." He nibbled her neck sucking on the pulse that exploded under his touch.

"It hurts."

"It will hurt, baby. Give me a chance." He was always begging with her.

She whimpered, and he held onto her hands refusing to release her.

"I've got you." He whispered the words against her ear.

Pulling back he saw her blue eyes staring back at him.

Slowly, he pulled out of her body taking his time and relishing every ripple of her pussy as she gripped him.

Donna gasped, throwing her head back as he released from her body until only the head was inside her.

Caleb took his time to slide inside. He wanted her to love this as much as he did. She winced, and he paused for her to get used to the feel of him.

"It hurts."

"Trust me, Donna."

"I don't know you."

He couldn't argue with her. Sinking into her warmth, he waited for her to accept him before sliding out. Over and over, he took his time thrusting in and out of her warmth. When she stopped wincing and her pussy grew slick with her arousal, he sped up his actions, going as deep inside her as he could. He didn't stop, and in no time at all, he was slamming hard within her core.

Keeping hold of her hands beside her head, he fucked her, taking possession of her lips as she cried out. He drank down every noise and moan she released.

"That's it, baby, scream for me."

Sliding a hand between them, he fingered her clit. She was attuned to him, and with a few strokes she came all over his cock.

"Fuck!" He yelled the word as her cum washed over his shaft and he felt each ripple along his length. Being without a condom was the best feeling in the world.

Claiming her lips, he fucked her hard, taking what he needed. His orgasm took him by surprise. Sliding inside her one final time he grunted out his pleasure.

Donna wrapped her arms around him at the same time as he held her, turning them to their side so he wasn't crushing her.

She was incredibly small compared to him.

Opening his eyes, he stared down into her face. She had her own eyes closed. His orgasm faded away. He didn't pull out of her body as he pushed some hair off her face.

"You're so beautiful," he said, causing her to open her eyes.

"Do you always talk afterward?"

"No. I don't stick around for anything afterward. I want to be around you." Her gaze went to his lips.

"Is it always like this?" she asked. She touched his lips, stroking her finger down his chest.

"No, it's not."

He didn't know what it was like for her, but she'd blown his world apart.

"You're going to be a little sore," he said. At least, he'd heard of women being sore after their first time. Touching her lip he thought about what Henry said. Was he prepared to lose everything because of her?

His first taste wasn't enough to satisfy this craving he had for her.

"I'm going to get you cleaned up."

****

Night had fallen several hours later, and Donna stood in his sitting room looking out of his window over the city. Bright lights and the sounds of passing cars could be heard. She'd opened the window slightly to allow some fresh air into the room. Caleb was on the phone in the other room, and she left him alone to give him privacy. Sipping at her soda, she twirled a strand of hair through her fingers. Glancing at her reflection in the window she wondered if she looked different. She felt different, but she didn't know if the whole world would be able to see the transition.

Sex, she'd had sex for the first time a handful of hours ago. It was a big deal, or at least it was a big deal to her. She didn't know what Caleb thought. Well, he couldn't keep his hands off her, so she must be doing something right. Resting a hand on her hip, she took another sip of her soda. After the first time together he took her into the bathroom where he'd made her soak in a long warm bath. He'd taken the time to add salts and get the water ready. When he joined her in the water she'd been so embarrassed she didn't know what to do.

Once their bath was finished he'd taken her into the bedroom and made love to her. His actions surprised her as she didn't have him pegged as the kind of man who'd make love. He fucked. Love never entered the equation with him, and she accepted that. She wasn't ready to settle down or to fall in love.

She didn't feel love for Caleb, lust maybe but certainly not love. There was no way she could feel anything for a man she didn't know and didn't really care to know. Tapping her finger on the can of her soda, she wondered what the hell she was doing. Nothing made any sense to her.

You're not a virgin anymore.

The second time Caleb made love to her, he took his time, loving every inch of her body until she couldn't think of where he ended and she began. One meeting in a jewelry store and she was standing in his apartment overlooking the city. "I'm sorry about that. Business needs to come first," Caleb said. She watched him approach her butt naked. Glancing down at her can, she tried to find any reason not to look at him or see him. What were they supposed to do with their lives now?

"No worries," she said. "What do we do now?"

She stopped asking questions as he wrapped his arms around her. His naked body pressed against her back, and he nudged her hair out of the way to kiss her lips.

"Should I go home?" she asked.

"No, you're not going home."

"I've got to feed my cat."

"You don't strike me as the kind of person to leave your cat without any food."

Donna hadn't. She'd put plenty of food down for her cat so she wouldn't starve.

He sucked on her neck, and his tongue licked along her pulse.

"I want to know what I'm supposed to do. This is unheard of for me." What was the proper protocol for them? Did she walk out on her own steam?

"Stop over-thinking everything you need to do." He turned her around to face him.

"I'm used to over-thinking everything," she said. She tucked some hair behind her ear as she glanced up at him.

He walked back into the sitting room. Gazing down his body she couldn't look away from the hard length of his cock. He was long and thick, pressing out toward her. In the low lighting, the tip glinted with his pre-cum.

"Then don't. I forbid you from thinking about anything but what we're doing." He sat back on the sofa and tugged her onto his lap. She placed her knees on either side of his legs, giggling.

"What are you doing?"

"You're not going home until tomorrow. You're in for one long night with me."

She didn't want the night to end.

Caleb didn't do love, nor did he do relationships. She could deal with the short term providing he kept his distance afterward.

"When we're alone, I forbid you to wear any clothes." He tugged the shirt she wore over her head, revealing her naked state.

Laughing, she dropped a kiss to his lips, moaning as he slid his tongue within her mouth. He cupped her ass spreading her cheeks wide. The curtains were open, but they were far enough up that the only way for people to see would be with binoculars.

He lifted her up, and she watched him grab his cock.

"What about the condom?" she asked, remembering protection for the first time that day.

"We've not used one."

She jerked, pulling away. "What?"

"I forgot to use one. We're safe, I promise."

Shaking her head, she pulled away from him. "No, we can't have sex. I can get pregnant, and you didn't even consider that?" She stepped away from him and grabbed the shirt she'd discarded on the floor. Her clothes were in the main bedroom. "I've got to go. This was a mistake."

One day of sex and she could end up with a child. The thought alone terrified her. Tugging on his shirt, she walked into the bedroom retrieving her jeans. She couldn't even wear panties as he'd destroyed him.

"You're overreacting," he said.

"No, I'm not. You're not the one who's going to end up saddled with a kid. I don't want a child, and you were wrong to forget."

You should have spoken up.

Tears filled her eyes at her own stupidity.

"Stupid, stupid."

"Look, nothing is going to happen. We're going to be fine," he said. His arms were spread out on either side of the door.

"Are you insane?" she asked. "Or are you just plain dumb? All it takes is one sperm, and should I remind you thousands of sperm are released during each orgasm, and all it takes is one." She held up her finger, glaring at him.

Anger took over, and she started to shake. Tying her hair back with the band she kept in her jeans, she whirled on him.

"Don't fucking speak to me like that," he said, growling out the words.

She flung her hand back and slapped him across the face. "You're an asshole and a jerk. You had no right to disrespect my body that way." The tears fell from her eyes, and she felt weak inside. She shouldn't let him see her pain. He didn't deserve to know how much he upset her. "You were the first man I was with, and yet you treated me like that."

Shoving past him, she ignored his aroused state even as pleasure gripped her.

"Donna," he said.

"No, don't Donna me. I've had enough. You shouldn't have done that." She opened his apartment door and charged down the long corridor. He called after her, and she heard him cursing. She imagined him grabbing a pair of jeans and trying to get into them.

Keep going.

Stepping into the elevator she saw him at the end of the corridor. The doors closed before he even made it to her. Tapping her hands together she waited for the doors to open once again. When they did, she charged out of the front door happy when Caleb was nowhere in sight.

Hailing a cab, she climbed inside as Caleb charged out of the building. She saw him, but he didn't see her. Sliding down the seat she blew out a breath, thankful he hadn't noticed her.

"Where to, love?" the driver asked.

She gave him her address then sat back. What the hell had happened?

Wiping the tears away from under her eyes, she forced all the bad memories out of her mind. Thinking of the negative wasn't what she needed to focus on.

It was over.

She must have broken some world record for breaking up with a man.

Get over it.

Traffic was a nightmare, and she didn't get home for an hour. She paid the cab and walked up the stairwell toward her door. Pearl was waiting for her. Closing the door, she bent down to pick up her cat.

"I'm sorry I left you for a man who didn't deserve it."

Locking the door, she walked back into her bedroom. Collapsing on the bed she didn't bother to change her clothes. "It was fun while it lasted, Pearl."

She doubted Caleb would be coming to see her any time soon. At least she hadn't told Lydia of her intention to go to him. All Lydia would do tomorrow was nag and try to get her to talk to someone else.

Closing her eyes, she rubbed her temples.

Her cat purred, and she chuckled. "Did you miss me?" Pearl gave her sad eyes. Letting out a breath, she cuddled up to her pet and closed her eyes.

She hoped she wasn't pregnant.

What Caleb had done was wrong. She should have made sure he wore a condom.

It's all your fault.

Pressing a hand to her stomach, she hoped nothing bad came of her mistake.

Chapter Seven

Caleb tapped his finger on his chair as Henry conducted business. It had been a week since the disaster with Donna, and he still couldn't get her out of his mind. This was dangerous. One week and he should be over her by now. He couldn't fuck any other woman either. None of them awakened a fire inside him the way Donna did.

"Why is the muscle conducting business, Caleb?" Elijah asked.

Glancing up, he saw the man opposite was staring at him. Elijah Weston dealt with the drugs. He was the man to talk to in order to get product moving out of the city to other states.

"Henry is very much a business partner. You're aware of this," Caleb said. He wasn't in the mood to be dealing with business.

"You can talk to me, Elijah. Caleb knows what he's doing even if he is being an ignorant ass," Henry said.

His friend was dressed in a suit while Caleb hadn't even tried to change. He wore a pair of jeans and a short sleeved shirt. Business wasn't all it was cracked up to be, and he was bored. The last week he'd dealt with work close to the club. Deals with alcohol, sex, and drugs were starting to wear on him.

"I don't care. I deal with one man, and that man is sitting and staring into fucking space as if he has a right to. I don't give a shit how your business works. I will fuck you both up if you don't get involved." Elijah slammed his fist down on the table.

Sitting up, Caleb leaned forward. "What shit do you actually need me to know? Huh? Do you want me to ask you how many people this will fuck over? Is it a white enough powder? I've got the cops. Just give us a fucking deal and sell us what you've got."

Elijah sat back. "You think it's that easy?"

"It's business. You've got shit you need to sell, and you know I can get the fucking job done. It's a win-win deal for both of us." Caleb stood, pulling out a cigarette. Staring out the window he saw semi-clad girls walking around weighing little white bags. It was the perfect little conveyor belt of pussy.

Donna entered his mind, and he closed his eyes, forcing her back.

"You think your smart assed attitude is going to get you what you want?" Elijah asked.

"I can take my money elsewhere, Elijah. We don't need you to make deals with us. Sell us what we want, or we go elsewhere."

Keeping his back to the other man, Caleb eyed up the women. Their dyed blonde hair and overly exposed bodies did nothing for him. He was going to go fucking crazy if he didn't get some kind of release soon.

Gritting his teeth, he listened as Elijah started talking money and sales. Within the hour they were ready for a shipment to the club and he was travelling alongside Henry toward Ecstasy.

"What the fuck is going on with you?" Henry asked. "We're a fucking team, and you've been fucking absent for the past couple of weeks."

"Nothing. Back the fuck off, Henry. I'm not interested in whatever shit you've got to say." He ran fingers through his hair. It was a Sunday night, and the city life was bursting with people trying to find an escape from their mundane lives.

"Back off? Back the fuck off. You've got to be fucking kidding me. Ever since you stuck your dick in that bitch you've been causing problems."

Without thinking he slammed his fist against Henry's face. The car swerved, and he lurched over grabbing the wheel. Drawing the car to the side of the road, Caleb opened the door and climbed out.

"You're telling me you've not got a fucking problem?" Henry asked, getting out of the car.

"Get back in the fucking car. I'm not in the mood for this shit." Holding onto the back of his head, Caleb stared up at the dark sky. He wasn't some limp dick virgin after his first pussy.

"You almost fucking killed us because of this need you have. Get your head in the game before you kill one of us. This only works because we're both on the same side." Henry spat the words at him, climbing behind the wheel. "Don't come back to the fucking club until you're ready to admit you've got a problem."

Leaning against the car, he stared inside at his friend.

"What if I need to keep her?" Caleb asked.

"Then you need to understand you're going to be putting her in danger. If you can accept that, then fine. I'm not going to say anything else. Step the fuck back from the car." Henry pulled away from the curb before Caleb moved away. He watched his friend go, then headed toward his apartment within the center of the city.

He kept his hands into fists, waiting for the moment someone tried to take him on. No one approached him. Slamming into his apartment block, he ignored the doorman and took the stairs toward his place.

Once inside, he went straight for the beer in the fridge. Uncapping the lid, he returned to stare out of the city life. Donna had left, and he'd not even tried to catch up with her. She was right. He hadn't respected her nor cared if she got pregnant. There were women who'd tried to get him take them without a condom, but he wouldn't sleep with those kinds of women.

How did he manage to get from one extreme to another? Some women would go out of their way to make him knock them up, yet Donna lost her shit over it.

Rubbing at his eyes, he tried to push all memory of her out of his mind. He couldn't. The few times they'd fucked she'd left a lingering mark on his soul. The tightness of her pussy, the sweetness of her touch would invade his thoughts when he least expected it.

Finishing off his first beer, he uncapped the second.

By the end of the night he knew he didn't have a choice. Tomorrow he needed to see her before he lost his shit and got either himself or Henry killed.

Collapsing onto the sofa, drunk, Caleb passed out.

The following morning, he woke up to the mess of the empty beer bottles around his apartment and a bad taste in his mouth. Stumbling into his bathroom, he stared at his bloodshot eyes and bad hair.

Stepping into the shower, he didn't wait for the water to warm up. The freezing cold would help to wake him up.

His mouth tasted like shit. After brushing his teeth three times and staying under the freezing cold water for half an hour, he climbed out and got dressed. His door was ringing. With a towel wrapped around his waist he opened the door to Henry.

"Is it okay to come in, or are you going to hit me again?" Henry asked, sporting a black eye.

"Shit, I'm so sorry. There's no excuse for what I did." He opened the door wider to let his friend inside.

"We got the delivery today. Have you thought about what I said?"

"I'm going to go and see her. I can't leave this alone." Caleb rubbed a hand down his face, blowing out a breath.

"Are you sure you don't just need another pussy to lose yourself in?" Henry asked.

"No other woman appeals to me. I'd have done it days ago if it would have worked." He started picking the bottles up.

"She's going to get us killed, Caleb."

Caleb shook his head. "She's not. Donna, she's different, man."

"That's the problem. She doesn't know this life. Cops sniffing around trying to make a name for themselves will go to her. You've got to let her know not to talk." Henry took a seat, pushing the bottles off his sofa.

"Let's take this one step at a time. You could help me," he said.

"Why would I help you? This is your mess. I didn't do anything." Henry leaned back in his seat, letting out a sigh. "You've got to love this life."

Rolling his eyes, Caleb picked up the bottles then walked into his bedroom and put on some clothes.

By the time he made his way back to the main sitting room, Henry had passed out on his sofa.

Deciding to leave Henry where he was, he grabbed his jacket and headed out.

Leaving his car in the parking lot, he took the time to walk.

Walking helped to clear his head and also gave him the time to brush off the drink. He stopped in a bakery to grab a coffee and a sandwich. When he got to the jewelry store, he was feeling revitalized and ready to face battle. It was after ten in the morning, and already the city was alive with activity.

Stepping up to the door he saw Lydia and Donna were inside.

His woman was at one of the glass cabinets in the corner away from the window with a chart in her hand. Her blonde hair was tied at the back, and her jacket was off showing off the white shirt and black skirt she wore. The uniform highlighted her fuller figure.

As he opened the door, Lydia looked up and glared.

He stepped inside and waited for Donna to turn around.

Seconds passed, and she looked over her shoulder. The blue of her eyes shot anger toward him.

"Lydia, deal with him, will you?" Donna turned back to her chart.

"Come near me, bitch, and I will hurt you," Caleb said.

He didn't give Lydia a second glance and walked up close to Donna.

"You're invading my space."

"I've given you a week to calm down."

She chuckled. "I'm not calm, Caleb. Leave before this gets ugly." Donna kept her head bent over the chart she was looking at.

She was pissed, but he was a master at getting what he wanted.

****

Caleb stood too close, and she was still pissed at him. Her traitorous body didn't care though. All her body cared about was how he'd feel pounding inside her like he had that one day they were together. Late at night her dreams were filled of him and only him.

He invaded her thoughts when she didn't want him there and pissed her off because all she wanted to do was forget about him.

Licking her lips, she pressed the end of the pen to her lip as she read the same set of numbers three times in a row. He hadn't moved away from her.

His large body covered her as he closed in around her.

"I'm not going anywhere."

She looked up at him. "What do you want?"

"Have you gotten your period yet?"

Glaring at him, she shook her head. "No, I haven't. Thanks for reminding me how much I hate you."

Pushing past him she signaled to Lydia that she was going in the back. Anything that put distance between them she was thankful for.

The door hadn't closed, and Caleb followed her through.

"You can't be here," she said, placing the chart on the table beside her.

"I'm not leaving."

"Let me guess, you're not leaving until you get what you want."

"It's the way I work."

Turning her head, she stared at the wall while she thought of what to say to him. "You're an asshole," she said.

"I know."

Gritting her teeth, she took a step away. "You're wasting your time."

"I can't get you out of my mind, Donna. I've been with a lot of women. I lost count of the number of women I've fucked and forgotten. I can fuck all of them, and yet none of them left me feeling like this." He placed a hand on the wall, trapping her against his body and the desk. "You're different. It has been a week, and I can't look at another woman without thinking about you."

"You used me. You disrespected me and my body." Tears filled her eyes as she thought about it. She didn't know if it was the right time of the month.

"Whatever happens I'll take care of it."

"I won't have an abortion."

"I wasn't suggesting an abortion. You're not killing any kid of mine."

Tears fell down her cheeks, and she wiped them away. "You don't get it. When I was going to get pregnant, I had every intention of being married and in love with that man."

He paused, staring at her.

"I know, it was a stupid, girly fantasy, but it was what I wanted." She laughed even though she wasn't finding anything funny. "My parents were in love. I wanted what they had, and you've taken that away from me."

She dropped her hands to her side.

"Donna?"

"No, you've taken that away from me because even if I'm pregnant I know you're not going to marry me, and not only that, I don't want you to marry me out of pity. There is no love between us, Caleb."

She backed away until the edge of the desk stopped her. He invaded the last few inches of personal space she had.

"I'll marry you if it will make you feel better. Don't shut me out."

"I don't want to be around you, Caleb. You're poison, and I can't have that in my life." He stayed close even as she insulted him.

Swallowing past the lump in her throat, he nodded.

"Fine. I'll give you space to work, but I'm not going away. I'll be here when you get off work at five." He wheeled around and left her alone.

Glancing through the glass partition she saw him leave the shop. Opening the door, she found Lydia waiting for her.

"What was all that about?" Lydia asked.

"He wants to see me again." She'd wiped the tears from her face before Caleb left. Lydia wouldn't know she'd shed a tear.

"Did something happen between the two of you?"

"No, nothing. He just wants to see me again. I'm going to finish work."

Turning back to the office, she picked up the file and started to work on the orders and mark up their products. Her hands were shaking from her encounter with Caleb. She didn't want anything to do with him even as her body did.

She knew he could make her scream and beg him for more.

Pressing a palm to her head, she closed her eyes and took several deep breaths.

"Think about something else, Donna. This is not the end."

When she was back under control she started to finish her work. At lunchtime she released Lydia out of the shop and stayed behind to eat her own food. The rest of the day went by uneventfully. Several people entered the store, and over half of them left without a single item to buy. She was used to people entering, looking around, then leaving. The jewelry store wasn't for everyone.

At five o'clock she dreaded leaving the shop. Caleb stood outside waiting for her. She and Lydia had already handed over the store to the other workers.

"You don't have to go out to him if you don't want to. Call the cops and tell them he's stalking you," Lydia said.

"It's okay. It's stupid to not face him." She offered a smile to her friend then took the lead exiting the store. "I'll see you tomorrow."

Lydia looked doubtful. Her friend didn't try to stop her, which she was happy about. Once she exited the store, Caleb threw the cigarette to the ground.

Saying goodbye to her friend, Donna started walking in the direction of her apartment.

"What do you want?" she asked.

"I've told you I'm not giving up easily." He stepped beside her, walking in time with her strides. "I know I disrespected you and your body. I want you to forgive me."

"I could be pregnant, Caleb." She stopped, turning to him. Poking him in the chest, she allowed him to see all the hurt he caused. "I didn't get a choice in that. You took that choice away from me."

"And I'm sorry. However, you're going to have to see that you need me here."

"Why?"

"That baby will be half mine. I'm not going to turn my back on my own baby."

His admission surprised her. "You'd stick by me for your baby."

"I've never been a dad. I've not got any wife waiting for me to come home. If you're pregnant then I'll put my name to him or her."

She leaned back. "Really?"

"Yes." He reached out to cup her cheeks. "I'm not going anywhere, baby. You've got me, and the baby has me for life."

"You don't mean that." She jerked out of his arms and started walking toward her apartment.

"I do mean that."

"You're a man who owns a nightclub. Shouldn't you have other women to bother?"

"No other woman has been a virgin, Donna. Not only were you a virgin but I did come inside you, twice."

Stopping once again in the middle of the street, she glared at him. "You have no right to say that to me."

Hitching her bag up on her shoulder, she turned away from him.

"Shit, Donna, look, I'm sorry."

"I don't want to hear it. All you care about is yourself."

He kept following her only this time he did it in silence. She wanted to slap him or at least hurt him. What kind of man did what he did?

What about you? Shouldn't you have asked about the condom first?

She'd been so naïve to trust him. When he'd given her a mind shattering orgasm and he climbed between her thighs, she'd assumed he put one on then.

Stupid!

Stupid!

Stupid!

All too soon she was outside of her apartment. With Caleb behind her she didn't reach for her pepper spray. He was far more threatening than any person within the building. Even she didn't want to mess with him.

She took the stairs as the elevator was broken.

He was still behind her as she placed her key in the lock and turned. There was nothing for her to do other than let him inside. He was far stronger than she was, and he'd already let himself inside once before using force.

Locking the door, she placed the key on the hook beside the door before walking straight to her kitchen to fill up the kettle.

Donna looked toward the sitting room to see Pearl sprawled out on one of her chairs.

"What are you hoping to achieve?" she asked, finally turning toward the man who'd invaded her life as much as he had her body.

Would a baby really be a bad thing?

She didn't think it would be a bad thing, providing he or she had both parents. Staring at Caleb, she didn't know the first thing about him and couldn't be sure if he'd stick around for any child they had.

"I want you back in my bed without waiting for you to leave it every chance you get." He folded his arms over his chest. Her gaze was drawn to all the ink he possessed. Again, did a standard businessman display his ink to the world? She must have watched way too many movies and stereotyped the perfect businessman.

"You crossed the line," she said.

"I want you in my bed. You may as well give me what I want, Donna. If you're knocked up, then there's no getting rid of me."

And they said romance was dead!

Chapter Eight

Caleb wasn't leaving without what he wanted. Today he was laying claim to Donna. He didn't know how long for, but Henry was right. She was messing with his ability to do his job, which wasn't good for him. The only way to survive in his business was to be always on his guard. With Elijah last night, he'd not been anything but careless and stupid.

He was willing to risk everything just for a chance to call this woman his.

"You can't be serious. This is your argument? I may already be pregnant so what's the point in denying us now?"

"I want you, Donna, and I bet that sweet, tight, pussy of yours, is dripping wet begging for me."

It was time to take matters into his own hands. Stepping closer, he grabbed her arms and walked her back until she was standing next to the wall. Running a hand down her body, he cupped her breast thumbing the hard nipple.

"Your tits want me. Your nipples are rock hard and aroused, Donna. It's not cold, and there's no excuse for this response." He glided down to the bottom of her skirt that fell at her knee.

Going under the fabric, he moved up. She squirmed in his hold. He wouldn't release her. Sliding the edge of her panties aside, he ran the tip of two fingers through her creamy slit. He was right. She was soaking wet to the touch.

Donna cried out, collapsing against the wall. If he didn't have his arm wrapped around her waist, she would have fallen to the ground. He wasn't letting her go.

"You can be angry at me, baby. I'll take your anger, your punches, I'll even take your smart mouth, but I will not let you go."

"I don't want you."

Thrusting two fingers inside her cunt, he watched her eyes dilate.

"You're lying. You want me even though you don't want to want me. There's a difference." Pressing his thumb to her clit, he rubbed from side to side. There was enough lubricant that it was easy for him to simply touch her. "Your mind may be telling you to push me away, Donna. This cunt, she's telling me another story. Do you know what she's telling me?"

She shook her head but he wasn't going to stop now.

"Your cunt is telling me to strip us both naked and fuck you right here, right now."

Releasing his hold on her, he tugged his shirt over his head. He stopped touching her, gripping the lapels of her shirt at the top and tearing open the offending item.

"What are you doing?"

"I'm going to do what I do best."

"What?" she asked. She tried to cover her body from his view. Caleb wasn't having any of it. Her body was all his to touch and play with. Unbuckling his belt and the button of his jeans, he shoved them down to his knees. Hiking up her skirt, he pushed her panties aside, feeling her silky warmth.

With one move he had her up against the wall, with her legs wrapped around him. He pressed the tip of his cock to her entrance and plunged inside.

Ecstasy. Being inside Donna was like taking a drug and riding the joy to an unspeakable high. Her cunt clutched him tightly, and her cream soaked his shaft.

"You're not wearing a condom," she said.

Gritting his teeth, he rested his head against her shoulder and slammed inside her once again. He couldn't pull out to grab a condom as leaving her tightness was out of the question. He knew he was being a bastard, but he couldn't stop.

"I'll wear one next time." He pressed his lips to hers, sliding his tongue inside. One hand was underneath her ass as the other went to her pussy. Caleb touched her clit, watching her head fall against the wall. Her eyes closed, and her mouth opened. "Come for me, Donna. Come all over my cock."

She shook her head.

Ramming inside her, he went as deep as he could. Each plunge into her cunt had her gripping him tighter than ever before.

"So fucking good."

Donna screamed as he stroked her clit. Her cum soaked his cock making it easier for him to slide deep within her core.

He kissed her lips as he fucked her hard against the wall. Caleb didn't stop as he plundered inside her. His tongue and his dick worked together to push her over the edge a second time.

When she screamed in orgasm, he groaned as his cum spurted inside her body. He rested his head against hers, not wanting to let her go.

"That was amazing," he said, groaning.

"Again, you didn't use a condom." She started to push him away.

He wasn't ready to be pushed away from her. Taking hold of her hands, he pressed them to either side of her head. His body and his cock inside her kept her propped against the wall. Holding her in place, he stared into her eyes.

"Let me go," she said.

"No. I'm not letting you go. You're mine, Donna." He was shaking. Something stirred in his gut, and all he wanted to do was carry her off to the bedroom.

"You're not being fair."

"I don't play fair. You wanted this, baby."

"I wanted you to wear a condom." She glared at him, tensing underneath him. When she tensed, amazing things happened to her cunt.

Gritting his teeth, he thrust inside her. "You better stop as otherwise I'm going to fuck you once again and you're not going to have any say in what I do."

He swiveled his hips giving her an idea of what he was talking about.

The time passed. He didn't know how long he stayed like that in the same position to keep her there.

Slowly, she started to relax, and the anger left her gaze.

"You're not a very nice person."

"I never claimed to be a nice person. You don't need to like me to want to fuck me." He released her hands and pulled out of her warmth. The skirt she wore was still hiked up around her waist.

He saw the white of his cum slid down her thigh. Did other men feel possessive when they saw that sight?

"You like that?"

"What?" he asked, thinking she meant the sight of his cum sliding down her thigh.

"The fact I don't love you or even like you."

Caleb shrugged. "I'm sure in time you'll change your mind."

He took hold of her hand and started to walk through her apartment. Pearl caught his attention as the feline stared at him.

Shaking his head, he opened one door to find her bedroom, and at the next door he found her bathroom. The apartment was small.

"How much do you pay for this place?" he asked.

She told him a sum that pissed him off. His woman was being ripped off. Donna was paying more money for a piece of shit apartment when she could be in a much better place.

He turned on the light and found the small shower room. Cursing, he turned on the shower to allow water to cascade into the stall. Turning back to her, he pushed the rest of her clothes off her body. Kicking off his jeans, he climbed into the stall, taking her with him.

"I can walk and do this myself."

"I'm not having you run from me or risk you calling the cops on my ass."

"I wouldn't do that." She stared him in the eye, and he knew she told him the truth.

"Then you're a fool."

She frowned. "Why am I a fool?"

"Most women to get rid of me would call the cops. They'd try to make my life as miserable as possible." He grabbed the soap from the shelf and started to wash her body. At first she started to fight him, shoving his arms away. Turing her against the wall of the stall, he trapped her in place. "Stop fighting me."

"No. You're a horrid person, and I don't want anything to do with you."

Keeping hold of her hands, he glared down at her. "I'm such a horrid person, yet I've done nothing to hurt you."

"You might have made me pregnant."

"But I've never hurt you. I could have hurt you that first night. I can take what I want. I've got you held against the wall with no way of you getting away." He pressed his point home by pushing his body against hers. "I'm not going to hurt you."

She stared into his eyes, and he hoped she saw the truth that he wouldn't harm her.

"Believe me."

"Why?"

"I need you to believe me." He trapped her hands against the wall, pressing his cock next to her stomach.

She sighed and shuddered beneath his touch.

Caleb tried to wait as long as he could.

"Fine, I believe you. What do you want?" she asked.

"Admit to me that you want me as much as I want you."

"I want you."

"Do you crave me?" he asked.

"Yes."

He kissed her lips, sliding his tongue inside her mouth.

"Then give us a chance, and I promise you, I'll wear a rubber, and if you're pregnant I'll do the right thing by you."

She let out a breath. He refused to look away from her and wouldn't back away.

"Tell me your answer," he said.

"Okay, I'll give us a chance, whatever this is."

Releasing her hands, he picked up the soap and started to wash her body. He'd won the battle, but he had yet to win the war.

****

Three weeks later

Lydia still hadn't quit her job in the three weeks Donna had been dating Caleb. Donna finished serving the latest customer, who'd bought an engagement ring. Glancing at the clock she saw it was a little after three. In an hour Caleb would be by to pick her up. For three weeks he'd been attentive and giving. There were times she forgot about the way they'd met or how he'd behaved. The fear of pregnancy was still there. It had been four weeks and she still hadn't gotten her period, but she'd never been regular.

After work she intended to go to the pharmacy to get a test. She hated not knowing, but, however, she didn't want Caleb to be there when she told him.

Their time together had been spent doing pretty mundane things. He took her to the pictures to watch the latest movies, and she spent a great deal of time at the club in the VIP section while he worked. Henry kept his distance from her. She didn't believe he approved of her involvement with Caleb. Donna did her best to stay out of his way. When she was at the club, Lydia and Darren joined them. She still didn't know the full extent of Caleb's business, but she'd seen the scars on his body.

Many of his scars were faded though some were still visible.

At night Caleb took his time bringing her alive. She had come to crave the nights when they were alone. He'd start by stripping her naked and kissing every inch of her body. Her cheeks heated as she remembered the way he opened her thighs and forced her to watch him lick her out. Caleb had taken a mirror and made her watch every moment of him devouring her.

Biting her lip she turned away from the window to glance at her friend. In the last three weeks all Lydia did was worry about her.

"Are you sure you know what you're doing?" she'd often asked.

The true answer was no, Donna didn't have a clue what she was doing? When she was with Caleb the whole world faded into the background until they were the only two people in the world. Even Pearl, her cat, adored him. Many nights they were curled up on the sofa with her cat on his lap, demanding he stroke her.

Gone was the vulgar man he once had been. She noticed he tried to keep himself in check around her. He didn't talk about his previous lovers or the women in his life. Donna learned not to ask, as he only ever evaded the question.

"Donna, I need to talk to you," Lydia said, putting her phone back into her pocket. The shop was vacant of any customers.

"Sure, what did you want to talk about?" Donna stood up and stretched out her muscles.

"Caleb, he's not all he seems."

"Lydia, don't. We've talked about this, and I know you're not one of his fans. I like him." She put her feet back into the pumps and wriggled her toes.

"He's dangerous, Donna. I wouldn't tell you about this if I wasn't worried."

She stared at her friend and saw the fear in her face

"What are you talking about?" Donna asked.

"I've been talking to Darren. I asked him to talk around. Caleb is not all he seems."

Donna stood and listened to what her friend had to say even though it was killing her to know more.

"He's a pimp, a drug dealing criminal." Lydia looked around the store. "He owns half of the city. He's the kind of man you don't want to fuck with."

"You're wrong."

Caleb couldn't be a pimp or drug dealer, could he? The bruises on his knuckles and the respect he gained wherever they were suddenly made some form of sense.

"No, he can't be. You're wrong." Donna shook her head even as she started to see things she wasn't sure were possible.

One of the nights she'd been sitting at the bar, she'd watched the barman hand a little white bag of powder to a woman who handed him a wad of cash. She had been going to ask Caleb about it when he'd appeared as if from nowhere taking her onto the dance floor.

"He used to be a fighter back in the day, Donna, and when he got older, he and his friend Henry started their own business."

"This can't be true," Donna said.

"Why can't it be true? What do you actually know about him other than the fact he owns a club? Nothing, you can't tell me anything. Darren found out more about him. He's bad news, Donna, and I think he's using you."

She shook her head. No, it couldn't be possible, could it?

"You're wrong."

Her cell phone started to ring, and she looked at the screen to see Caleb's name. He'd bought her a cell phone when he discovered she didn't have one. She'd never had a cell phone as she'd never needed one. Why buy something she didn't need?

"Is that him?"

Answering the call she put the phone to her ear. "Hello," she said.

In the background she heard a lot of men grunting. Frowning, she turned away from Lydia so her friend didn't see her expression.

"Hey, baby. I'm not going to be able to pick you up. I'll pick Chinese up and stop by your place tonight."

"What's the matter? How come I can't come to you?" she asked.

"I've got work, babe. I'm sorry, but I'm going to have to go." He hung up before she could say anything else.

"How are you so sure?" Donna turned back to Lydia.

"Darren is never wrong. He's been to a couple of the illegal fights. Don't tell him I told you that. It's not hard to start hearing gossip."

Changeover was in less than ten minutes. Donna grabbed her bag and looked at her friend. "I've got stuff to do. Is it okay if I leave you to finish up here?" she asked.

"Donna, I don't think you should go looking for him. He's bad news."

"He's my bad news. I need to know what's going on." She quickly put her jacket on and hitched her bag on her shoulder. "Are you good here or not?"

"I'm fine. Go."

Turning her back on Lydia she walked toward the door. She didn't give herself a chance to think. Hailing a cab outside, she gave directions to Caleb's club then sat back to think about everything Lydia had said.

Pimp.

Drug dealer.

Fighter.

None of them made sense, and yet they did. What was going on with him?

He sported bruised knuckles, and he'd yelled a lot down the phone. Henry always kept his guard up around her.

It had to be true. There was no other explanation.

"Here you are, love."

Glancing out of the window she saw Ecstasy's sign on the doors. The club was closed, but she saw some of the staff cleaning up the crap outside.

"Could you stay here? I don't know how long I'm going to be."

"Sure, doll. It'll add to the price."

"No problem." Climbing out of the car, she walked up to the door. For several seconds she stared wondering what the hell to do. When she couldn't handle the curiosity anymore, she opened the door and walked inside. She saw the bartender cleaning glasses and chuckling with a brunette dressed in a skirt that didn't even cover her ass.

"Donna, can I help you?" he asked.

She couldn't remember his name even though Caleb had told her.

"I want to see Caleb. Where is he?" She tucked her hands in her skirt pockets and blanked everyone else out.

The bartender visibly tensed. Did they know who he was?

"He's out at the moment, busy. Can I take a message?"

Glancing at the brunette, she saw how the other woman looked at the counter. Did everyone know who he was but her?

"Yeah, tell him not to bother coming around tonight unless he's prepared to tell me the truth." She turned on her heel and made her way out of the club.

The bartender called her name, but she ignored him. As she climbed back into the cab, her whole world felt tilted on its axis. Her gut had told her to stay away from him.

She'd ignored her gut, and now she was panicking.

Paying the cab driver, she climbed out and walked toward her door. She was inside her apartment and closing the door when her cell phone went off.

Rejecting the call, she placed her keys on the hook and tugged her jacket off. After a quick shower, she changed into a pair of jeans and a shirt. When she looked at her cell phone she saw over ten missed calls along with a dozen messages from him. Deleting them all, she tried to ignore the phone.

Caleb was not the kind of man to be ignored.

When her phone rang for the twentieth time, she answered, ready for him.

"Donna, what the hell is going on? I said I was bringing Chinese home and yet you're going to the club. What's going on?"

"Who are you?" Donna asked.

"I haven't got time for this shit. What the fuck is going on?"

His anger wasn't hard to miss. She chuckled. "Are you a pimp? Do you deal drugs? Are you a criminal? These are the kind of questions I've got for you."

Silence met her questions, and her gut twisted.

"Who told you?" Caleb asked.

"So it's true? All of it?"

"I'm not discussing this shit with you over the fucking phone. I'll be there tonight," he said.

"Don't bother. I don't want anything to do with you." She hung up, and when the phone rang again seconds later, she launched it against her wall. Donna watched the device shatter on the floor.

The silence was a blessing and a curse. She didn't want to be hearing anything yet knowing her life was never going to be the same again.

Caleb had invaded her life, and he'd destroyed it at the same time.

She'd given her virginity to a pimp.

Closing her eyes, she fisted her hands and tried to ignore the pain of what had just happened. What had just happened?

Had she fallen for a criminal?

Caleb didn't do love, but that didn't stop her from falling in love with him.

Pressing her face against her hands, Donna started to sob. She'd fallen for a man who'd kept his true identity from her. What was she going to do?

Chapter Nine

Trying Donna's number again, Caleb knew she'd either smashed the phone or turned it off. Whoever was responsible for telling her the truth was going to deal with him.

"Trouble in paradise?" Henry asked.

"Someone told her who I am." He turned back to the man they were punishing for trying to sell coke on their turf. Caleb had caught him last night trying to roofie one of the women in his club. He was one of Drake's cronies trying to wheel in on his turf and piss him the fuck off.

"Who would have told her?"

"The only person she listens to is that friend of hers." Looking at Henry, he came up with a plan. "Go to her place and get rid of Darren."

"Darren?"

"Yeah, that fucker is running his big mouth about the fights. We can't have a loose mouth on our turf. When you're done, threaten the friend and get back to me." Caleb ran a hand over his face.

"This is covering shit up, Caleb. This is where mistakes start to be made."

"I don't give a fuck what mistakes are being made. I'm repairing some damage caused. Think about it. Darren talks to the wrong fucker, the games are invaded by cops, we all lose."

Henry let out a sigh. "Fine, I'll go and deal with this shit. What about this fucker?" Henry pointed to the man who was close to death any way.

Pulling out his gun, Caleb fired, shooting the man in the head. Henry stepped back.

"Clean the mess up. I've got shit to do."

Without waiting for someone to stop them, he left the warehouse and walked to his car.

"This is a mistake," Henry said.

"Look, it's been a month that I've known her, and I'm not giving her up."

"There's other pussy around, Caleb. You don't need to settle for the first one who spreads for you." Henry stood with his arms folded.

"I've tried to fuck other women. I don't expect you to know what I mean. This is different. Donna's different, and when I'm around her, I forget all the other shit." He ran a hand over his face.

"Three weeks is not enough time."

"Three weeks in the ring could have us dead or put us on the map. Three weeks can cause problems and solve them. It doesn't matter about the time, Henry. It's about feeling. Shit, I don't expect you to understand." He opened the car door and made to climb inside.

"Just remember she can be used against you. Come clean or find a really good lie." Henry tapped the hood of his car, and Caleb pulled away.

Driving toward her apartment he didn't think about anything else. He forgot about the food, and he parked up in the only available parking space. To get to her apartment, he'd broken the speed limit.

Running up the stairs taking them two at a time, he banged on her apartment door.

"Let me in, Donna."

She didn't answer, and he banged on the door again. He wasn't going anywhere.

"Go away," she said, shouting through the door.

"No, you've got to let me in to talk to you."

"There's nothing to say. Please leave."

Gritting his teeth, he slammed his fist on the door. "Open the fucking door before I smash it the fuck in."

The door was opened, and she stood staring at him. There were no red blotches around her eyes from crying. She looked ready to hurt him.

"What do you want?"

He pushed his way into her apartment closing the door behind him. She didn't scream at him, only stepped back.

"We've got to talk."

"You're not the man you said you were."

"I never said I was anything." He ran a hand down his face as he looked at her.

Her gaze was on his hands, and he saw what she saw, the knuckles with bruises and blood on them.

"Who are you?" she asked.

"I'm Caleb Cassell."

"I know your name. I also know that you own the club with Henry. What I don't know is everything else." She folded her arms, glaring at him. The shirt rode down exposing a great deal of cleavage. He'd woken up and sucked on those tits. Caleb had yet to fuck her tits and ass, but he was going to.

"Are you pregnant?" he asked. He'd been waiting impatiently to find out the truth.

"I don't know."

"It's been a month, and you've not started your period. I'm not stupid, Donna. You're pregnant."

"I've never been regular in my life. It doesn't mean anything, and I've not taken a test to confirm yet."

"Why do you keep hiding from the truth?" he asked.

"Why do you keep lying to me? I've told you the truth about who I am."

"I can't tell you the truth unless you agree to marry me," he said, firing out the ultimatum.

"What? That's absurd." She glared at him, her beautiful blue eyes promising fire and danger. "Why can't you just be a man and tell me the truth?" Donna yelled, opening her arms and standing close to him.

She lashed out, slapping him around the face. He accepted the first blow, but by the third, he'd had enough.

Grabbing her arms he tackled her to the ground.

Donna cried out, screaming for him to leave her alone. He wrestled her to the ground, and he rested between her thighs.

"Fucking stop. You're going to hurt yourself. I'm stronger and fucking faster than you." He yelled the words against her ear to force her to stop.

"You're a monster."

"I'm not. I'm a fucking businessman." She wriggled underneath him. His cock responded to her body moving underneath his. For a split second he enjoyed the feel of her body against his.

"You sell women. I can't believe I gave myself to you." She tried to force him off. Donna wasn't a match for his strength.

"I protect women who want to sell their fucking bodies." He snarled the words at her. The last thing he regretted was being with her. The past three weeks had been sheer perfection to him. There was nothing he'd change about being with her.

She called to him. Her sweetness gave him hope that he could have something more meaningful in the future with her.

"What?" she asked.

"I've never claimed to be a good man. To the world I own Ecstasy. No one needs to know the rest. I worked in an underground fighting club. I learned to keep my fucking mouth shut and fight. Fighting was where I met Henry. We couldn't fight to the death all of our lives, and so we took off on our own."

She stopped moving to listen to him.

"The club is a front to sell the drugs, but I keep it fucking clean. This is my business, and I need you to keep your mouth shut. This world, it's not safe." He stared into her eyes. "Now, I'm going to release your hands, and you're going to keep those fucking claws to yourself, understood?" he asked.

Donna nodded.

He released her hands and leaned back, giving her plenty of room to move. Slowly, he climbed off her and helped her to her feet.

"I'll tell you what you want to know, but then you remain my woman, Donna."

"You can't do that."

"It's simple. You want to know the truth, you find out knowing you're not having another man in your life. I'm it for you, baby."

"I can date whoever I want."

He shook his head. "No, I'll kill any man who thinks he can touch what's mine. You're mine, Donna."

"That's not your decision to make."

"Babe, it was made the moment you let me inside your fucking cunt. I don't share, and there's no way you're taking another man."

She tucked some hair behind her ear, and her hands were shaking. Guilt swamped him at what he'd done.

"You better tell me the whole truth then," she said, taking a seat on her sofa.

He watched Pearl climb up on her lap.

Sitting in the chair opposite he leaned on his knees and gave her his full attention.

"What I'm about to tell you can never leave this room."

"I've got no one to tell," she said, staring at his hands.

"You can't talk to Lydia either. This is dangerous."

She visibly swallowed then turned her gaze to his. "Then I won't tell anyone, but I think it's time I find out who I share a bed with."

He told her everything and didn't leave anything out. Caleb opened up about his life from the fighting down to the change with Henry where he became his own boss.

"You're the boss?" she asked. "You have the final decision?"

"No and yes. Henry has a scar down his face, and he doesn't like to deal with the front of the business, so I take that role. We let others believe that I'm the one in charge while he's simply my guard. It's not the case. He's my best friend, and I won't let anything happen to him."

His cell phone buzzed, and he looked down to see it was Henry.

Henry: Deal's done and brunette is up to speed.

"So, you're not the boss?"

"I help decide shit, Donna. I don't pass that buck along to Henry. I'm in this with him."

"Why can't you stop and do other things, legal things?" she asked.

"I could. It doesn't earn me enough money to do what needs to be done. If I wasn't running this, someone else would. Those women, they came to me because another guy was roughing them up and forcing them to take drugs. I don't force anyone to do shit they don't want to do." He pocketed his cell phone. "All of the women, they can leave when they want. I don't force them into the lifestyle. This is their choice, not mine. I'm the muscle to take care of them. A lot of men try to rough them up, and I stop them."

"I just can't believe this is true." She stared down at her cat.

"You can't tell anyone. If you call the cops then you're dead. There's only so much I can do to help you."

"I could die for knowing this about you?"

"Yes."

"I won't tell anyone. I don't want to die."

He saw the tears start to fall. Going to his knees in front of her, he tilted her head back.

"You're under my protection, and I won't let anything happen to you." He pressed a kiss to her lips, surprised when she didn't pull away. "I'm going to go to the pharmacy to get that kit. Stay here and don't let anyone inside."

"I won't."

He stared into her eyes to make sure she wasn't lying. Convinced she'd do as he asked, he got up and took her keys. She wasn't going to risk her life. Even the cops would give him the head's-up if she turned up at the station.

Leaving her apartment he called Henry.

"Everything clear on your end?" he asked.

"Yeah, Lydia's going to keep her thoughts to herself. It helped she had a shit load of bills. We paid them off and put some cash in her account. Darren is out of the question. I went to see him, and the fucker pulled a gun on me. I didn't have a choice, and he was going to shoot Lydia. I've paid to clean away the body, and Lydia won't say anything. She looked pretty pissed he was using her as a shield. It's probably a good thing he's gone. He'd been talking to too many people. Fucker didn't know when to keep his mouth shut, but he does now."

"Lydia's not going to cause us problems, is she?" He was done with problems for tonight.

"No, she won't. I've told her plain and simple, keep her mouth shut or get a bullet in the head. She's decided to stay silent." Henry cleared his throat.

"What is it?" Caleb asked, rubbing his eyes.

"I've told her not to say anything to Donna. She's to tell her that Darren broke up with her and left town. Your woman won't know the truth of what went down or that we interfered to make him go away."

"Thanks, man, I appreciate it, but I'm going to tell her the truth."

"Are you sure about that?" Henry asked.

"Yeah, I'm sure. Thanks for taking care of the problem."

"Anytime."

Hanging up the phone, Caleb climbed behind the wheel. Now he needed to find out what was going to happen in his life.

****

Donna sat on the toilet seat with the bathroom door closed. She heard Caleb pacing outside of her door. His movements continued to unnerve her. Closing him out of her mind she focused on the white stick in her hand. She was shaking so bad she could barely see the section that was about to determine her fate. Was she pregnant?

Would she be able to love her child?

The very question had her in knots.

"Baby, you can't keep me out," Caleb said.

"I've asked for these few moments. Please, let me have them." She closed her eyes, and when she opened them, any hope she had dropped.

She was pregnant with Caleb's child. Tears welled in her eyes, and she stood up, going to the door.

He stood holding onto the doorframe as she opened it up.

"I'm pregnant," she said, glancing at the stick then handing it to him. Brushing past him, she went into her bedroom and climbed on top. Holding onto a pillow, she closed her eyes and tried to blank out the fear that was clawing at her.

I'm going to be a mother.

The very thought seemed foreign. She heard Caleb in the background along with the rustling of paper. He was probably reading the instructions to make sure she didn't fuck up.

Stop thinking.

She couldn't stop thinking or feeling. Her life was going to change, and there was nothing she could do to stop it.

The bed dipped behind her. In the next instant his arms were sliding around her waist. "You don't need to worry," he said.

"I'm not going to stop worrying. I carry a life inside me. In case you didn't notice, it's a huge deal." She kept hold of the pillow, treating it like a lifeline or at least a security blanket.

His fingers pushed her shirt aside, and he started to stroke her stomach. "We'll get through it."

"You're a pimp and will probably end up in jail. I'll be forced to bring this child up on my own." All of her fears multiplied in the face of what she was going through. The tears fell down her cheeks silently.

"I'm not going to jail. I always watch my back, Donna. No one can pin shit on me. I'll be part of our baby's life."

She liked the way he touched her stomach. The slow caresses helped to calm her nerves.

"I'm sorry," she said.

"You don't need to be sorry. I'm the one in the wrong. I should have told you the truth in the beginning when you asked. This is all on me." He kissed her neck.

She kept her eyes closed wishing for a few moments that things were different. Growing up she always imagined she'd be married when she got pregnant. This just went to prove that life never went how she imagined. Blowing out a breath, she opened her eyes to stare at the wall opposite her. There was no magical answer to help her decisions.

"What are you thinking?" he asked.

"I don't know what to do. This is not how I expected to be pregnant. I always expected to be married and have been in a relationship a few years, not weeks."

She sniffled as the emotions suddenly weighed down on her. Life truly wasn't fair.

"I'll arrange for us to get married. Do you want to be married in a church?"

Shaking her head, she tightened her hold around the pillow she was holding. "You don't have to marry me. I'm pregnant with your baby. You're not in love with me."

"I care about you, Donna. Some couples don't even have that much going for them." His breath fanned against her ear. Closing her eyes, she waited for him to finish talking. With him close behind her, she couldn't deny the attraction. Her body refused to listen to her mind, and she heated, wanting more from his touch.

Squeezing her legs together, she waited for the pleasure to stop, but it only increased.

It wasn't fair. He only cared about her while she was falling in love with him.

"What have you eaten?" he asked.

"Nothing. I couldn't stomach food."

"I'm going to nip out and get some food. I'll be back before you know it." He dropped a kiss to her head and climbed off the bed.

She waited until she heard the door to her apartment close and lock before reaching over to grab the phone beside her bed. Dialing Lydia's number she waited for her friend to pick up.

"Hello," Lydia asked, sniffling.

"Lydia, are you okay?"

There were sounds over the line, and she heard a male voice in the background.

"Why are you calling?"

"I needed to talk to you. You're my friend, Lydia."

"I'm sorry. I don't mean to be a bitch. Shit, Darren broke up with me." Lydia broke down, sobbing across the line.

"Honey, I'm so sorry."

"It's okay, really. He told me I wasn't good enough, and he just upped and left. The bastard."

She listened to Lydia curse and rant about her current boyfriend.

"I can't believe he did that to you."

"Well, I bet he was cheating on me. I'm going to the health clinic for a checkup and test. I don't want to get any diseases. Bastard couldn't keep it in his pants." Lydia blew out a breath, laughing. "What about you? Why did you call?"

"Erm, I'm pregnant."

"What!"

"I know. Caleb went and got a test. I'm knocked up." She watched Pearl enter her bedroom and jump up onto the bed.

"Are you happy about it, or are we sad?"

"We're … I don't know how to feel about what's going on." She smiled and stared down at her pillow.

Pearl nudged her hand out of the way and sank onto the pillow. She stroked her cat rather than her pillow.

"Is he happy about it?"

"He's gone to get some food. I think he's going to marry me. At least, he's talked about marrying me." She shrugged, knowing that Lydia couldn't see her. "He's not run off yet. I guess I'll see."

"Maybe you'll be the woman to change him."

"I doubt I'll change him. He's set in his ways."

Lydia mumbled her agreement. "About today, I think it's best that we don't talk about it ever again. I'm not interested in pissing anyone off."

"I think that's a good idea. Lydia, you don't have anything to be afraid of."

"I know. Erm, I'm going to go and have a wash. I smell."

Chuckling, Donna said her goodbyes and hung up the phone.

Stroking down Pearl's back, she sighed. "I don't know what's going to happen. I can't believe I'm pregnant, and now I'm talking to my cat hoping you'll tell me what to do."

Life was passing by so fast, and if she wasn't careful she wouldn't have gotten a chance to live.

When her door opened she climbed off the bed and went in search of Caleb. He held a box of Chinese.

"I got all of your favorites."

For three weeks he'd been learning everything about her.

"Thank you. I'm starved." She smiled, tucking some hair behind her ear.

"Come and sit." He walked into her small kitchen area. She owned a small dinner table only suited to two people. He opened the correct cupboards in her kitchen and pulled out two plates. She watched him navigate her area as if he had an intimate knowledge of her space. "I'm going to start looking into getting a house. Our apartments are not suited to raise a kid." He placed an egg roll along with noodles and sauce onto a plate. She took it from him and the chopsticks from his hands.

"Do you want me to come with you?"

"Yeah, we'll pick a place together."

Eating some noodles she looked up at him and wondered what to think. Four weeks ago he walked into the jewelry store to get a bracelet for a woman he was going to end a relationship with.

Now, she was pregnant by him, discovered he was involved in criminal activity, and about to move in with him.

He joined her at the table.

His legs brushed hers, and he reached out to take her hand. She stared at his fingers then placed her hand within his.

"We're going to get through this, Donna."

"Lydia called, and she said Darren has left her." She watched his jaw tense.

"Baby, I've got to tell you something."

Donna listened as he told her everything that happened with Darren, Lydia, and Henry. Tears filled her eyes as she thought about her friend being held with a lunatic who had a gun. "Why would she lie to me?"

"You're her friend, and Henry was trying to protect me. He knows how important you are to me. I'm not going to do it. I won't keep secrets that involve you. Lydia's your friend."

Donna nodded. She understood both points. She still felt weak and exhausted from their fight.

Nodding, she took another bite of noodles. Caleb changed the topic of their conversation.

"We'll start looking tomorrow for a place. I'll pay, and I'll make the necessary arrangements for us to be married."

"You don't need to marry me."

"I'm going to marry you."

Donna looked up to see him staring at her. "No man is allowed to touch me?"

"Yes."

"What about you?" she asked.

"I'm not going to be touching any other man," he said, smirking.

"What about women? You've told me often enough that you've been with other women. I want to know whether you'll be faithful or not."

He stared at her. "And if I say no?"

"Then we'll bring a child up together, but you won't be touching me. I can't do it, Caleb. I'm not going to be the kind of woman who turns her back."

"There won't be any other woman," he said. "You're the only person I need. The only person I'll ever need."

He squeezed her hand.

Was there any way for her to believe him?

She ate her food knowing in her heart and mind that she didn't have much of a choice. Her only option was to believe him, as otherwise she wouldn't be able to cope with such an uncertain future.

Chapter Ten

Time passed slowly, and Caleb took the time to look for houses to arrange their wedding. Lydia and Henry both agreed to be their witnesses. Donna refused to have a big wedding, and she didn't want a honeymoon either. Looking for a place to live was also proving to be rather difficult, or the truth was, Donna was being difficult. The places they'd visited she found something wrong with them.

The rooms were too small, the garden too dangerous or the price too steep. He was patient knowing he was taking her out of her comfort zone. Henry wasn't sticking his nose in to shit that didn't concern him, and work was moving by peacefully. He hated the peace. In his line of work he knew something big was going to happen, but he didn't know what.

Thinking about his friend, he was reminded of the time he'd told Henry he was going to pay a visit to Lydia. Henry had gotten angry and told him to leave shit well enough alone.

In all of his life, he'd never been able to leave shit alone. Taking a visit to her place one night he found Lydia alone. He warned her what talking would do. She wasn't going to be telling anyone. The thought of losing Donna or his kid because of someone running their mouth filled him with fear. He couldn't lose either of them. When he was at the club late at night, his thoughts would always return to Donna. She was his reason for continuing on with his life.

She gave him a reason for fighting another day to keep the bad shit at bay. The rumor mill was running riot with news of his upcoming wedding. He employed a guard to keep Donna safe whenever he wasn't there. She didn't know she was being followed, but he'd always been overly cautious. As the days passed, turning into weeks, she stopped being so cold toward him. Last night they shared his bed, and she didn't push him away. He felt closer to her than ever before.

On the thirtieth house when Donna found more than three reasons not to live there he lost his temper. When the realtor left the room he turned on her.

"What the fuck are you doing?" he asked.

She turned toward him. "I'm not doing anything."

"Every house we've been to is a problem. I want to know what your game is. Are you going to wait until you're ready to drop to pick a place or are we going to go around in circles?"

Donna looked at the floor. He saw the red in her cheeks.

"You were."

"No, I mean yes. Erm, I didn't want you to make a rash decision." She tucked some hair behind her ear. "Buying a house is a huge deal, and I'm not going to be able to be part of it. This is your decision, but I don't want you to come home one night hating the fact I've stolen you away from your life."

Staring at her, Caleb tried to see if she was telling him the truth or lying. "This is all about me?"

"Lydia told me you're not the man to settle down. This was before you told me the truth. I don't want you to think that I got pregnant on purpose." She was fidgeting where she stood.

Reaching out, he cupped her cheeks. "Baby, I'm the one who forgot protection. If anything, I don't want you to hate me." He pulled her within his arms. "I've been giving you time to get accustomed to me."

"You've not touched me, Caleb. Ever since you found out about me carrying your child you've been cold toward me." Tears filled her eyes, and he watched them fall. He wiped her tears away.

This was all a big misunderstanding.

"I've been giving you space, baby. Fuck, if I'd known you wanted me I'd have been on you sooner. After everything we've been through I didn't want you to think I was using you."

She smiled. "You were being sweet?"

He chuckled. "Yeah, don't tell anyone. I lose my mind when I'm around you. And I've got a hard rep to keep up."

Wrapping his arms around her, he stroked her cheek.

Donna opened her mouth then closed her lips. He wondered what she was going to say before she stopped.

"Pick a house, baby."

"This one."

"Are you sure?"

"Yes. I like the size and the garden." She rested her head against his chest. "I think this one is perfect."

Stroking a hand down her back, he inhaled the scent of her. This was heaven to him. He couldn't live without her, and he needed to keep her close to him, protect her.

"Can we go back to your place?" she asked.

"We can go back to my place. I'll go and speak to the realtor." Cupping her cheek, he dropped his head and kissed her lips. "Go and get in the car."

He joined her in the car after he dealt with the house. Donna was sitting waiting for him with some soft tunes on. Caleb didn't waste any time heading toward his apartment. Henry was in charge of business while he spent time with Donna.

She didn't speak as he navigated traffic. His cock was rock hard at the chance of being with her. Tapping his hand on the wheel he tried to think of something else while the time passed. All he could see was the beauty of her cunt open for him.

"Did you like the house?" she asked.

"Yes."

Would she be wet for him? Every time he touched her, she melted against him even when she tried to be cold toward him.

"I want you, Caleb."

He chanced a glance toward her. She rested her head on the seat and smiled.

"Baby, I'm holding on by a fucking thread here. Tell me if you're being serious."

"Yes, I want you." She let out a little moan. "What have you done to me?"

"I'm not going to complain." He parked up at the underground parking facility. In quick time he had her out of the car and was escorting her toward the elevator. He didn't waste any time in talking to the security guard.

The elevator ride took so long that he thought he was going to lose his mind. He held her arm as he made his way down the long corridor. Inserting the key, he opened the door and closed it by pressing Donna up against it.

"Tell me this isn't what you want and I'll stop," he said. In his mind he was begging for her to tell him to continue.

"I don't want you to stop."

"Tell me to fuck you." He pushed the jacket she wore from her shoulders.

"Fuck me, Caleb."

Growling, he tugged her close and started to tear at her clothes to get her naked. He needed to feel her close against him.

"Please," she said, moaning. Donna attacked his clothes, and for several minutes they were all hands and mouths as they moved together across the room. He was careful not to hurt her, taking his time as he moved into the bedroom.

Stepping out of his jeans, he watched her wiggle and remove her underwear. There was no real sign of her pregnancy yet, but that would come within weeks. He looked forward to seeing her with a rounded bump showing off his child.

"Fuck, Donna, I need you. It has been too damn long."

She charged at him, circling his neck and dragging his lips down to hers. "Please, no more talking. Take me, fuck me."

Dropping her to the bed, he crawled up the bed and opened her thighs. He stared at the perfection of her pussy staring up at him. She was slick, her cream coating the fine hairs covering her lips.

"Caleb?"

"Shh, I'm going to taste this pretty pussy of mine."

He opened the lips of her sex to see her clit swollen glinting at him, begging for him to suck.

Sinking down onto his front, he licked the creaminess of her slit. The taste of her exploded on his tongue. "So beautiful." He muttered the words against her pussy.

Caleb sucked her clit into his mouth, biting her clit, then smashing his tongue against her nub. She cried out and thrashed underneath him. He held her down with his grip on her hips as he tongued her pussy.

"Please ... please ... please ..." She begged him over and over again. He loved hearing the sounds from her.

Sliding his tongue into her core, he plundered her warmth, drinking her down.

He changed his movements, first plunging into her core then sliding up to stroke her clit. Caleb moved up and down, drawing her closer and closer to orgasm. His cock was rock hard. The tip of his cock leaked pre-cum over the sheets. He was desperate to be inside her.

Forcing himself to take his time, Caleb dined on the sweetness of her cunt. She thrust up to his waiting tongue, and he licked her out, drinking down her cum.

He flicked his tongue over her clit, and she splintered apart in his arms. Holding her down, he forced her into a second orgasm before he released her body. Pressing a kiss to her clit, he smiled up at her.

"Do you feel better, baby?" he asked.

****

"Yes, I do." Donna had been waiting for him to make the first move. She didn't know what to do to get him to see that she wanted him. Did she go to him or wait until he made the first move? Did he even want her now that she was pregnant with his kid?

Nothing made any sense to her. He kept his distance when they were looking at the variety of houses. She felt like he was there in person but in his mind elsewhere. Watching him crawl up her body, she smiled down at him. He had this look on his face that made things inside her tighten.

"If you ever need me I'm always here and prepared to do whatever needs to be done for you." He rested between her thighs.

When he kissed her lips, she licked her cream from his chin, moaning as she did.

"Do you like the taste of yourself?" he asked.

She nodded, kissing him back.

He ran his hands down the side of her body going to her hips. He plundered her mouth with his tongue. Opening her mouth, she accepted him inside, whimpering as he rubbed against her. The length of his cock was between the lips of her sex rubbing up and down. He bumped her clit making her gasp.

Caleb kissed from her mouth down to her neck then back up again. "God, I love the taste of you."

She whimpered as he continued to bump her clit and send the pleasure shooting through her body. "Please, Caleb, fuck me."

He reached between them, and she watched him grip his cock then place the tip at her entrance. Lying back, she stared up into his eyes. Dark eyes that had once scared her now made her feels things that terrified her. Over the weeks they'd been together, house hunting, getting to know one another, she'd somehow managed to fall in love with him. When no one was around to witness them together, Caleb was one of the nicest, sweetest men she knew.

Slamming in deep, he groaned as she gasped. He was so deep within her that it took pleasure to a completely different dimension.

"Donna, I love you."

His words took her so completely by surprise that she stopped thrusting up against him and stared. "What?"

"I love you. I've loved you from the first moment I saw you." He pushed the hair off her face. "I want this, baby. I want you in my life, with my ring on your finger as my wife." He kissed her lips, sliding his tongue into her mouth.

"You're being serious?" she asked, pulling away.

"I've never been more serious in my life. I know my line of work is dangerous, but your protection is the most important. I will take care of you and look after you for the rest of our lives."

"What are you trying to say?"

"I'm asking you to marry me, not just because you're pregnant but because you love me and you want to be with me as much as I want to be with you."

She smiled, cupping his cheek. "I love you, Caleb."

He took her lips in another searing kiss before she could say anything else.

"I know I don't deserve your love, but I promise you I'll work for the rest of my life to make it better for you. I'll make up for the mistakes I've made."

Donna pressed a finger to his lips. "Shut up and kiss me. I don't need anything fancy from you. All I need is you." She leaned up and kissed him, sliding her tongue into his mouth at the same time as she held him close.

He pulled out of her body only to slam back inside her.

She whimpered, breaking from the kiss to moan.

"That's it, baby. You're so fucking beautiful," he said. "Come all over my cock." He glided a hand down her body to stroke her clit.

Wrapping her thighs around him, she went to the peak within seconds sliding into oblivion with such ease.

"So perfect," he said, fucking her harder than ever before. There was no stopping him as he climbed toward his own orgasm. She held him close as he grunted, his cock jerking within her as his seed pumped deep inside her.

When it was over, he didn't pull away, but he tugged her close holding her tightly.

"I can't believe you love me."

"Not only do I love you, Donna, you're in here," he said, pressing her hand to his chest. She felt his heart beating rapidly against his palm.

"I don't want to know about your other businesses, Caleb. Providing you stay safe and come back to me, I don't wish to know about anything else," she said. She'd thought about it long and hard. Donna loved Caleb the man, not the pimp, drug dealer, or whatever the hell he was into.

"Then I won't tell you about it. I'm not going to hide what I do from you, though." He took her hand within his, and she gave him a squeeze.

"Okay," she said, snuggling in against him. Running her fingers over his chest, she smiled.

He may not be all that perfect, but he was perfect enough for her. Even men with dubious lifestyles deserved to be happy.

Epilogue

Five months later

"She's the one then?" Henry asked, coming to stand beside him. Caleb glanced at his friend before returning his gaze to the woman standing beside Lydia. Donna's rounded bump stuck out from the dress. She was six months pregnant, and for once in his life something was actually going right.

"Yes, she's the one. The only one." He'd not even looked at another woman since he'd laid claim to her. Caleb attended every appointment at the doctor and the hospital. Her care was his main priority.

"Don't know how you can do it. I'm into fucking everything with a nice warm hole and a willing scream."

Caleb shook his head. "You'll find a woman soon. I'm sure of it."

"With this fucked up face, I doubt it." Henry took out a cigarette and lit it up.

"I'm not going to talk about this."

He'd seen the way Lydia and Henry looked at each other when no one else was watching. His friend was into something. Caleb didn't know what, but he'd bet money it was because of her.

"Whatever, man. I know I'm happy with the woman I'm with."

"Not going to change who I am for anyone." Henry saluted him before walking away.

Heading toward his wife, Caleb wrapped his arms around her waist, stroking his son or daughter within her stomach.

"Hey, baby," he said, kissing her neck. He noticed Lydia tensed at his company. They'd not gotten past him threatening her yet. Maybe in the future it would be different. He liked the fact she was afraid of him.

"Congratulations on this big day," Lydia said.

"I'm stealing my wife away." Without waiting for Lydia to say anything he escorted Donna onto the dance floor.

"That was rude," she said, smirking.

"What? I can never get my wife alone anymore. It's a curse." He closed his eyes as he held her against him. "I love you."

"I love you, too."

The songs kept on playing, and Caleb didn't care if it was an upbeat one or a slow one. He was leading his woman into a slow dance of love and life. Resting his head against hers, he breathed her in. "Do you have any regrets?" he asked.

"None, you?"

"No."

She melted against him. Closing his eyes, Caleb knew he'd do everything in his power to feel this way about his woman.

****

"Leave me the fuck alone," Lydia said.

Henry smirked, standing on the edge of the dance floor watching his friend dance. "I'm just standing here."

"You're a monster."

Still smiling, he sparked up another cigarette. Lydia was his one problem. Five months ago he'd killed her boyfriend in front of her and threatened to kill her as well if she didn't keep her mouth shut.

Staring at Caleb, he started to wonder who was the bigger monster between the two of them. Caleb had fallen in love while Henry was in love with his guns and implements of torture.

"Then run away," he said, glancing at the brunette who kept pissing him off. She was the bane of his existence and had been since she'd begged him to spare Darren. Henry didn't believe in second chances.

She folded her arms and stood beside him.

"I'm not going anywhere."

Interesting. Lydia pretended to be scared of him and then stood beside him as if she didn't have a care in the world.

"Okay, Princess, let's see how long that bravery lasts."

Placing his arm along her shoulder, he waited to see what she did.

When nothing came, he was as confused as he was over five months ago. What was it about her?

The End

DEDICATION

As always I want to thank Evernight for their constant support and also, Karyn, my lovely editor who is always patient with me.

SAM CRESCENT

THE SCARRED ONE

Deadly Duet, 2

Sam Crescent

Copyright © 2014

Chapter One

Henry fisted the whore's hair as he pumped his dick into her waiting mouth. The good thing about paying a woman to suck his cock was they never complained about how dirty he wanted it. He loved it when a woman took him to the back of her throat and swallowed down every inch she could. Sometimes they gagged, and other times the women just took what he gave them without complaint. This woman, she was good, an expert in taking his thick cock. The woman between his thighs had dyed blonde hair and a nice pair of fake tits that didn't fit into his palm. The whole package was a disaster. She wasn't anything he wanted, and yet if he closed his eyes to the suction of her lips and imagined another woman, he was close to orgasm.

Staring at the ceiling for several seconds he tried to stop himself from imagining *her,* but it was a struggle. He thought about her long brown hair wrapped around his fist. In the last few months she'd grown out her hair, and it was lovely and long. He'd seen the waves caressing down her body when she visited Donna. Caleb wouldn't allow his woman to be cut off from her friends even though Henry had advised him to keep Lydia out of all the problems. Would her brown eyes be bored or filled with fire as she took his cock?

Fuck, his thoughts when it came to Lydia were driving him insane. There was nothing special about her. She was chunky, mousy, and entirely boring compared to the woman swallowing his dick.

But even as he thought about the boringness of Lydia, he couldn't stop from thrusting into the woman's waiting mouth and spending himself between her waiting lips. She swallowed down his cum, moaning as she did.

She's paid to like it. Lydia would never be paid.

Opening his eyes, he stared at the white ceiling. Caleb had had several decorators in last week to do a nice job of this part of the club. Ecstasy was a club he and Caleb owned together. They were known as the "deadly duet" with him being referred to as "the scarred one". They held a good portion of the drugs, girls, and guns within the city and were their own bosses. Together they made a living out of everything illegal while using the clubs they opened as a front. Ecstasy was one of the places where they distributed to the public. They'd met many years ago when they were both fighters. Neither of them believed they were going to last as fighters, and so their business interests expanded and they were now two of the most feared crime lords in the city. Currently they were in talks with another man, Elijah Weston, who owned drugs all over the country. They were hoping to get together to expand their distribution, and maybe go overseas.

"How was that, baby?" the woman said, smiling up at him.

"Fine." He got to his feet, pulling up his pants and securing his belt into place.

"You're going?"

"I'm not interested in seconds."

"Yeah, I've heard that about you." The woman sighed, taking a seat on the bed. "All the girls said you were the love and leave 'em type of guy."

"I don't waste my time on pussy that's known more cocks than a fucking lavatory. You're a fucking whore, and I don't need to waste my fucking time with you." He threw some notes down on the bed, hating the fact he'd used another whore. His reputation was starting to piss him off when it came to the whores who worked at Ecstasy. He didn't like the fact he was becoming known amongst the women. Without looking left or right, he made his way back to the main part of the club. The blowjob hadn't done what he wanted. He was still tense and ready for a fight.

"Get me a fucking beer," he said to a passing waitress and sat down in his usual seat. Caleb was coming back with Donna from the dance floor at the main part of the club. Henry didn't like how happy the two fuckers were.

He stared around the room wondering what the hell to do with the rest of his night. Usually he spent the night fucking one of the whores until he kicked them out to finish sleeping. He wasn't interested in fucking anyone or anything for the rest of the night. One blow job would have to do for the night. Henry didn't know why he was so pissed off about the time he spent with the whores who worked for him, only that he was.

A soft voice interrupted his thoughts, forcing him to turn to see Lydia walking up the steps toward the table. She held a drink in her hands, which she placed on the table. "I'm sorry about that. Your barman, Richard I think his name was, kept flirting with me. He wouldn't leave me alone."

Richard was one of the new men that Caleb had hired a few weeks ago. Henry was looking into his references as he thought there was something off about the fucker.

"Be careful, he might end up like your last one," Henry said, glaring at her. He didn't like Richard. The bastard was too fucking arrogant for his own good, and Henry just didn't like him. Henry had watched the other man sneer at the whores and turn his nose up at some of the waitresses in the last few weeks, as if he was better than everyone else. No one was better. They were all fucking equal. Now Richard was flirting with the best friend to the boss's woman. Many of their associates didn't know Henry was partners with Caleb. Henry liked it like that. It was the added element to their partnership that people didn't expect. Ever since Caleb had fallen for and married Donna, however, Henry had attended more meetings on his own. He didn't like it even as he understood what was going on. Donna wasn't an awful woman. She was sweet to the core, and that, as far as he was concerned, could cost them in the long term. Once their enemies realized Caleb had a weak spot, they were going to go after her.

Sleeping with the whores meant Henry didn't have to worry about anyone or anything.

Lydia glared at him, sipping at her drink.

He stared at her, waiting for her to say something. She did not, averting her gaze away from him. The fact she wouldn't growl at him or get angry pissed him off. She'd been there when he'd had to kill her boyfriend. He'd been the one to clean up the mess alongside her while she cried.

"Did he ask for your number?" Donna asked.

"Yeah, but I'm not going to give it to him. I don't know him."

"You don't want to appear too desperate, do you?" Henry asked.

Again, she glared at him without giving him anything else.

"It's time you started dating," Donna said.

If he heard any more he was going to get his gun out and start shooting. He wasn't interested in women's shit.

"I'm not ready. I'll start dating when I'm ready."

"Don't leave it too long. Your pussy will dry up and you'll be next to useless," Henry said, barking the words at her.

"I'm going to the bathroom." Lydia got to her feet, continuing to glare at him as she passed. He didn't care and stared right back at her.

Donna followed her.

"What's your problem?" Caleb asked once the women were out of earshot.

"Why do you have to bring your woman here? She's vulnerable here, and shouldn't she be at home caring for your son?"

Donna being at the club also bought Lydia along with her. Considering the two women didn't work together anymore, Henry had assumed they would pull apart. Donna no longer worked as she and Caleb had a young son at home. Lydia worked as a receptionist at a hotel chain. She worked the morning shift. He knew, as he'd followed her.

"Donna deserves to have some time out. I asked her to come with me to the club. She's my wife, Henry. Be careful how you speak about her."

Holding his hand up in surrender, Henry shook his head. "Fine, consider myself out of it."

"You're being a prick again. The whores not giving you satisfaction anymore?" Caleb asked.

"My trip to the whores was more than fine." He saw the waitress approaching their table. "It's about fucking time," he said, taking the beer from her. She stuttered something that sounded like an apology. "Fuck off."

"Okay, seriously, whatever's bothering you, you've got to stop. The club is not your ground to piss people off. I'm always having to replace our staff or give an excuse for shit behavior, and I'm not in the mood to be pissed with, Henry." Caleb glared at him as he spoke.

"You're not the one doing all the employing anymore. I'm the one doing all the shit while you play fucking husband with your girl. I'm not interested in hearing you moan." Lydia and Donna cut off more of what he was going to say. "Fuck this." Henry snatched his beer off the table and stormed off. Henry refused to listen to Caleb any longer.

Leaving the table and the VIP area he made his way toward the bar, securing his own corner.

****

"Don't let Henry bother you. He's always a little mean," Donna said. They were standing in the bathroom, and Lydia washed her hands under the tap. She knew how mean Henry could get. She'd witnessed that cruelty at first hand. Lydia hated the man. He was rude, abrasive, and cold. There was not any redeeming quality about him, yet she remembered him kneeling beside her as she scrubbed the blood off the floor.

Cutting the memory off, she dried her hands and waited while Donna did the same.

"I won't let him bother me." Lydia ran fingers through her hair, trying to put some order to the long length. Lydia had let the length grow out in the last few months. "Let's not talk about him anymore. How is your son?"

"Luke's a dream, and I swear, Caleb would do anything for him."

She'd changed the subject in the hope of luring Donna away from talking about Henry. The scarred man terrified her. The coldness in his eyes always sent a shiver down her spine. Only once had she seen him look different, and that had been at Donna's wedding. There had been something dark, almost alive within his gaze. Unlike Donna, Lydia wasn't in the dark when it came to Caleb and Henry. Both were bad men, criminals of the highest order. Darren, before he was killed, had told her everything about the Deadly Duet. They were known for being a team, and anyone who tried to take them on ended up dead.

Darren didn't leave anything out of his description of the two men. No, she wasn't intrigued by the scarred man. He scared her.

Leaving the bathroom, she listened to Donna talk about Luke and Caleb together. She didn't know how much Donna knew of Caleb's business. Lydia wasn't stupid. Caleb had warned her to keep her mouth shut or risk being dead. She had a shit life, but she didn't want to lose her life by opening her mouth to tell the truth.

Back at the table, she watched Henry get to his feet and leave. She blew out a sigh of relief that was short lived as Caleb tugged Donna into his lap.

Sitting at their table feeling like the third wheel, Lydia took a sip of her soda. The barman had tried to get her to buy something alcoholic, but she refused. She was no longer drinking alcohol. Every time she drank, she took a man home who she later regretted having in her life. In her search for love she'd met too many toads.

There was no Prince Charming for her.

Out of the corner of her eye she saw Caleb was stroking up the inside of Donna's dress. Lydia's drink was empty, and she needed an excuse to get away from the couple. Their love made something clench deep in her gut. She didn't need her own lack of love thrown in her face.

"I'm going to get a refill." Getting to her feet, she left right before Caleb attacked Donna's mouth.

Her friend was chalk to Caleb's cheese, yet they were both totally in love. She stepped around the table, giving them as much room as possible. On the way to the bar she paused when she saw Henry was drinking alone. The only space was right next to him as the bar was filled with people lingering for a chance to get in on some action. Closing her eyes, she counted to ten then headed toward him.

She placed her glass on the counter, trying her hardest to ignore the man beside her.

"What are you doing here?" he asked.

"I'm getting a drink. Do you have a problem with that?" She glared right back at him. Lydia wouldn't let him scare her. After everything she'd seen, she refused to let him see how much he unnerved her.

He wasn't the one to pull the gun first.

No, Darren, her now deceased boyfriend, had been the one to pull the gun first and almost get her killed. If it hadn't been for Henry reacting fast she wouldn't be here now. God, he'd been so quick to draw his weapon and take out Darren.

"I've not got a problem with that. I've got a problem with you still being around when you're not wanted. Can't you take the hint and leave?" he asked.

"Why are you being so rude? I've never done anything to you." She fisted her palms, wanting to hit him. There was no need for his attitude.

"This is who I am."

"Our friends are married. I know you hate me, but you've got to learn to be civil." She rested her hand on the counter, turning to face him. His gaze ran up and down her body.

"Stop checking me out." She didn't like the thrill that rushed through her at the interest in his eyes.

"Baby, I've got plenty of pussy on hand." He took a sip of his alcohol. The glare from the bar's light illuminated his face, showcasing the scar down the side of his face in harsh light. "I don't need or want your fat pussy. You're not the right woman for me. I like my women slender."

His words cut her hard. She'd never been good at saying no to food and could afford to lose several pounds, but she never got around to it.

"Hey, honey, can I get you anything?" the barman asked.

What was his name again? Richard? She couldn't remember.

Her chest was hurting from Henry's cutting remarks. Tucking some hair behind her ear, she shook her head. "No, thanks. Erm, it's time for me to go. Could you tell Donna I'll see her another time?" She didn't give either man a chance to respond.

Lydia walked out of the club, taking in the warm air as she started walking down the street. It was late, dark, and the noise from the city was loud. Henry's words kept rolling around her head, and she couldn't make any sense of them. She rubbed at her chest. Why did they have to hurt? It wasn't like he was the first man to call her fat and he sure wouldn't be the last man.

The pain was something she didn't understand. She'd been called fat or other names for a long time. Yeah, some men liked her, as she was pretty, but it had been a long time since they were intentionally cruel like Henry had been.

"Shit, Lydia, stop," Henry said, invading her thoughts. She glanced over her shoulder to see he was walking to catch up with her.

She didn't stop walking. The last person she wanted to be around right now was Henry. His cruelty knew no bounds. She'd done everything he asked after Darren got himself killed, and yet it still wasn't good enough for Henry. When was he going to leave her alone?

"Fuck, you sure walk fast," he said, walking in beside her.

"What? I walk fast considering I'm a fat person with a giant ass?" She didn't even look in his direction. He was the last person she wanted to see.

"Look, I'm sorry."

"Don't apologize to me. I don't need to hear any words coming out of your mouth. I understand that you're a cruel man, but I feel sorry for the other women. Oh, that's right, they're your whores. They're paid to overlook your disgusting language and general hatred for our sex." She didn't know why she kept talking, but she couldn't stop. "I'm not being paid to stay in your company, and I refuse to be a near a man who's so mean and horrid." She folded her arms over her breasts, trying her hardest to block him out.

"I'm really sorry." He grabbed her arm, and she pulled away from his touch.

"You don't get to touch me."

Henry held her purse up. "You forgot this."

She snatched her bag from him without saying a word. "Are you done? You can go back to your women. You know, the ones you pay to keep you happy?" She started walking away again.

Why are you angry?
You hate Henry.

This makes no sense, and you're starting to sound like a crazy person who doesn't know what she's talking about.

If she wasn't careful she was going to start talking to herself, and that would be too embarrassing.

"Wow, I think that's the most you've spoken about in the last couple of minutes." He held her still. They were stood at an entrance to an alleyway that would lead to where she lived.

"Ugh, you're an insane, crazy, horrible man. You're a murde—"

She didn't get to finish her insults as he covered her mouth and pressed her up against the brick wall. "You've got to keep your fucking mouth shut. I mean it, Lydia. It's fucking dangerous to be going and opening those lips of yours."

Once again his touch awakened the desire in her body, and she hated him all the more for it. She'd seen how dangerous he was firsthand. There was no way she'd ever trust him enough to get close to him.

He released her face, and she stared at him, waiting.

"Don't speak words you don't understand."

"I know what I saw," she said.

"Seeing is not fucking knowing. You and I both know that bastard you were fucking would have killed you. I saved your life. I deserve a little fucking respect."

"You're mean and cruel."

"And I'm never going to change, so stop taking what I say personally. I don't think about what I fucking say, I never have. You're beautiful, and you should already know how beautiful you actually are." He cupped her cheek, surprising her further.

"I hate you."

"Good. You don't even know me." He took a step back.

She went to open her mouth to growl at him some more, but the squeak of tires interrupted her.

Henry glanced toward the sound as a van with blackened out windows pulled up beside them on the road. "Fuck, run, Lydia."

Three men poured out of the van attacking Henry before he got to his gun. She watched the weapon fall to the floor as they started to hurt him. Instead of running, she threw herself at them, hoping to stop them from hurting him. She hated violence in all forms.

She was no match for them, and neither was Henry. One of the men slammed his fist against the side of her face and slammed her against the brick wall. Everything suddenly went black.

Chapter Two

Henry groaned as he opened his eyes. Fuck, he must have drunk too much last night and gotten into a fight.

"Great, you're awake."

He knew that voice. What the fuck was Lydia doing near him? Lifting his head up, he groaned at the sudden explosion in his head. The events of the previous night swarmed him, and he sat up taking in his surroundings. Last night he'd not recognized any of the men who'd attacked them. They'd gotten to him before he could draw his weapon. Henry had lost his temper when he saw one of the men attack Lydia.

Glancing around him, he saw he was on a bed with one of his hands tied to the headboard.

"What the fuck?" He saw Lydia was sitting with her hand bound in the same position as his, and they were both on the same bed. There were a couple of lights in the musty smelling room.

"Yeah, my thoughts exactly." She rested her head back, and he saw the dark purple bruise on her cheek.

"Fuck, I'm so sorry."

"Do you even know who did this or why?" she asked, rolling her head toward him. "My head is really hurting, and I stink."

"No, I've not got a clue who they are or what they want." His head and ribs were killing him. One of his hands was free and he lifted his shirt to see the bruising spreading across his chest and stomach. He'd put up a fight, but three against one had been insane odds to win. Henry winced at the pain.

"Are you okay?" she asked.

"Yeah, I will be. I've had a lot worse done to me before."

"They were not exactly friendly, were they?"

He kept staring at her face. When he got his hands on the man who hurt her, he was going to kill him.

"No, they weren't. Does it hurt?" he asked, reaching out to cup her bruised face.

"It hurts everywhere. He threw me against the wall."

The low lighting made it a nightmare to look, but he wanted to check her out in case she had any internal bleeding.

"I want you to shuffle off the bed and stand up. Lift your dress up and show me where it hurts," he said.

"I'm not getting naked for you to mock me."

"I won't mock you. I need to know that you're okay. Please, do as I ask."

"No, I'm not showing you my fat body." She glared at him, the fire spitting at him from her brown eyes.

"Look, you're not fucking fat, okay? I said some mean shit to you to get you to leave. You're not fat. You're perfect. Now hike your dress up so I can see if you're hurt." He'd been mean on purpose. The scent of lavender had invaded his senses the moment she stood beside him in the bar. He didn't like how easily she affected him. Seeing the barman who didn't have a single scar on his body or within his body, Henry had lashed out. Men like Richard the barman could have whatever he wanted. For so long he'd been satisfying his need with faceless whores whom he paid to give him what he wanted.

Jealousy.

The emotion had taken him completely by surprise, and he hated how vulnerable it made him.

"You're not serious."

"I'm deadly serious. I got rock hard from seeing you in that dress, and believe me, I'd come inside a whore's mouth twenty minutes before I saw you." She groaned, looking sick. "Yeah, I know I'm disgusting, but this is who I am."

"I don't need to know about your sex life. I've never been mean to you."

"You tried to break Donna and Caleb up."

"She was innocent to everything he's ever done. I was looking out for her. Why can't you see that?" Lydia asked. "You've hated me from the moment you shot and killed Darren. This has nothing to do with me."

"Just stand up and show me your fucking body so I can stop worrying. I don't want to have to be on Caleb and Donna's shit list because you're dead."

She growled but did as he asked, moving to the edge of the bed. He saw her stand and slowly work her tied hand across the headboard.

"You better keep your nasty as shit comments to yourself." She reached across her body and started to work her dress up her body.

He was a horrible man as he started to get aroused. She wore silk stockings and suspenders that went to her mid-thigh. The small black panties settled over her crotch, and he would have given anything to see if she was bare or had a small thatch of curls. She was turning him the fuck on with need.

Lydia presented her back to him. "Well, can you see anything?" she asked.

He'd not been paying attention. The panties she wore were in fact a thong. The thin piece of material nestled between the cheeks of her ass, and he'd give anything to be that small piece of fabric. Forcing himself to look away from the tempting curves, he checked out her back. She was badly bruised from being thrown against the wall, but he couldn't see any signs of her bleeding or damage. He was no doctor, but through his years as a fighter, he'd learned some valuable lessons.

"Well?"

"You're fine. It's going to hurt like hell. You're bruised."

She dropped her dress, and he wished he'd given her another reason to keep it hiked up. Slowly, she moved back into the space on the bed.

Silence fell between them. Staring at her feet, he saw her stockings hadn't survived the attack or the kidnapping.

"What do you think they'll do?" she asked.

"I don't know who they are or what they want." He glanced at her, wishing she'd turn to look at him.

"You're so calm. How are you not losing your shit?"

"This isn't the first time something like this has happened. About five years ago I was screwing a whore in one of the towns where Caleb had started up some new contacts. I didn't pay attention, and she was a lure to get me vulnerable. I was taken for three days. Caleb struck a deal, got me out, and we killed the bastards for taking me. This is not new to me. They'll tell us what we want, maybe even try to scare us. Don't worry, it'll be fine."

He tried to reassure her, leaving out the part of the torture they'd dished out to pass the time. Henry really hoped they left Lydia alone. He didn't want her to get hurt.

More silence followed, and he took the time to listen to what was happening. He heard people walking around upstairs, so the bedroom had to be in the basement. There were no windows to speak of, and that gave another clue that they had to be underground.

"Do you think Caleb will find us?" she asked.

"Yeah, he'll find us."

With his free hand he searched his pockets to find them empty. Not surprising really, it meant they'd kidnapped people before, but how far would they go with him?

He looked down on the bed to see her hand opening and closing into a fist.

"Are you nervous?"

"No."

He reached over and placed his hand over hers. "Stop."

"Okay, I'm nervous. I've never been kidnapped before, and I'm scared. I don't want to die." Tears filled her eyes, and they cut him to the core to see.

"Lydia, I promise, nothing is going to happen to you. I won't let it."

"I wouldn't make promises you can't keep." The door to their room opened. Henry didn't release Lydia's hand, but he took his time to see there was a set of steps that led upstairs. Two men entered the room, closing the door behind them.

Henry didn't recognize them either.

"I can keep promises. You don't need to hurt her," Henry said. Both men were dressed in classy suits. Neither of them spoke of being associated with a lowlife criminal or gang.

"We'll do what we think is necessary." One of the men stepped forward. His hands were behind his back, thrusting his chest out. Henry looked from one man to the other, trying to figure out which one was in charge. He wasn't stupid. A lot of their business associates thought he was dumb, but he acted that way so they wouldn't take him too seriously. He always had his and Caleb's best interests at heart.

Leaning against the headboard, he watched them both. He wouldn't be the one doing all the talking. They'd kidnapped him, and he wasn't going to give them anything.

"I'm sure you're curious as to why you're here?" the man in front said.

Henry stared, waiting for them to continue.

"I don't think he's listening." This came from the man behind him.

Lydia stayed tense beside him. He was pleased she hadn't started begging for her life or sniveling. There was only so much he could take.

"I'm not the one who wants to chat, boys," he said, smiling between the two men. "You were the ones who were impatient and took me off the street. I'm waiting to see what you've got to say."

"You're Caleb Cassel's bodyguard, Henry."

No one was ever interested in learning his full name.

"So?"

"So, we're interested in a deal going down between your boss and Elijah Weston."

Okay, drugs. That put them in one category. They were dealers themselves and didn't like being cut out of the deal. He could handle this, but it would also require Caleb and Elijah.

"There are a lot of deals going on. You're going to have to tell me which one upsets you."

"Who's the bitch?" the one in the back asked.

"What's your name?" Henry asked, looking at the man nearest him. He didn't want any of them looking at Lydia. She was not part of this, and he was going to do everything to stop them from looking at her.

"Why should we tell you?"

"You know my name, and yet I can't know the man who kidnapped me off the street. It wasn't nice, by the way. You suck at kidnapping. Now, if you'd been nice to me we could have discussed this properly." He released a sigh. "Whatever, talking's for pussies."

"I'm Leon, and that's Bill." Leon was the man closest to the bed. "Now, tell us who the bitch is."

"She's my whore." He tightened his hand around her so she'd get the message that he was working.

"She sure doesn't look like one of the whores you frequent. She's too homely looking," Bill said, staring at her.

He didn't want any of them looking at her.

"She's got a nice tight cunt, ass, and mouth. It's all I need." He looked at her, knowing she was cursing him with every second that passed. "Now, how about we go upstairs and discuss this like normal people. Being tied to a bed is creeping me out."

****

How dare he treat her like that?

Lydia fumed as she looked around the room. She really needed to use the bathroom, but Leon and Bill had taken Henry the bastard out of the room. No one was with her, and she was tied to the bed.

Whore!

God, the only reason she hadn't called him out on it was because of the way he held her hand. This was Henry's job, his business. She was not related to this kind of business in any way. Blowing out a breath, she pressed her legs together. She really needed to pee, and it was getting harder for her to focus on anything else.

Minutes passed, and when she could no longer stand the pain of needing the toilet, she started to shout.

"Hey, I've done nothing wrong. I deserve the chance to go to the toilet." She waited to see if her words drew any attention. Nothing happened. Frustrated, annoyed, and desperate, she started to scream.

Finally, the door opened, and she saw Bill glaring at her.

"What?"

"I really need to pee." The glare on his face made her wish she hadn't started shouting. Without Henry around, she didn't know how to react or what to do.

Bill charged into the room. He grabbed her arm roughly and released her hand from the bind on the bed. She tried to rub her wrist, but he tugged her across the room toward the door. He practically dragged her upstairs.

"Your whore wanted the toilet." Bill threw her to the floor in front of Henry. "Well, she's your bitch, deal with her."

Lydia made to get to her feet, but a gun pointed at her head made her pause. She stared up at Henry, but he was staring at Bill.

"What the fuck are you doing?"

"I'm not a bitch. You take her to the toilet and deal with her." Bill's cruel voice told her he was going to do something more.

"We're waiting for Caleb to get here for this deal to go down and you want to waste my time with her pissing?"

The humiliation was complete.

"I don't give a fuck. We're the ones in charge here, not you. Show the whore how to be treated."

A shiver worked down her spine. This was not going to go well.

"Come on, get up," Henry said, reaching down toward her.

"No, a whore doesn't get to walk around. Make her crawl to the toilet."

"I'm not going to make her crawl to the toilet."
Henry folded his arms glaring.

"She's a whore. She either crawls like the whore
she is or I shoot her in the head. I'm not bargaining with
Caleb for your woman. I'm bargaining with your boss for
business." Bill pointed the gun at Henry. "Now make the
bitch crawl."

Lydia stared up at Henry in time to see him grit
his teeth.

"Come on, bitch, you heard the man. Crawl."

This was the worst night of her life. She really
couldn't remember a time she'd been more humiliated.

Closing her eyes, she forced the tears back as she
slowly crawled her way, following after Henry.

"She's one fat whore. I did hear you weren't right
in the head with all your scars." Bill kept taunting, and
there were several other men to witness this degradation.
Every second that passed Bill kept throwing more insults
her way. "There's the bathroom. Hurry the fuck up.
You've got no chance of escape, so I wouldn't even try
it."

Still crawling on the floor she waited for Henry to
open the door before she made her way inside. Once the
door was closed she slumped down and covered her face
with her hands. The situation she was in finally hit home.

"Come on, don't let them do this."

Lydia sobbed into her hands, wishing something
was different. She hated what was happening.

Henry pulled her hands away. He was crouched
down in front of her. The concern was easy to see on his
face. "Do not let them win this, Lydia. We're going to get
out of this alive."

He was whispering, and so she whispered back.
"You don't know that."

"I know we're going to get out of here alive. Now, go to the toilet before they start to test me."

"I don't want to go in front of you." She was mortified at the prospect of him listening to her pee.

"Baby, I've heard a lot worse in my time than a piss. Come on, go to the toilet." He helped her to her feet.

"Thank you," she said. Her cheeks were red hot from embarrassment.

"Please, don't worry, Lydia. Take a piss and then we'll go out there and face them all together."

She glanced up to see him facing the wall.

Removing the stockings she threw them in the corner, no longer wanting them on her body. She had wanted to feel sexy when Donna invited her out. Lydia hadn't been with a man since Darren, and she wanted to connect with someone.

The last person she expected to be connecting to was Henry. A few hours ago he'd insulted her, and now she was finding him sweet.

Get a grip on yourself, Lydia.

She sat on the toilet covering her face with her hands as she relieved herself.

"Why do you work at a hotel?" Henry asked.

Dropping her hands, she stared at his back. "What?"

"I was just curious why you left Dreams, the jewelry store, when you were making good money."

"The risk of getting robbed is a lot higher in Dreams. After Donna left because of her pregnancy and living with Caleb, I didn't see the point in staying." She'd been to a couple of jobs before landing the one as a receptionist in a hotel chain. The work wasn't challenging while some of the clients were rude, disrespectful, but at least she wasn't at risk of being terrified.

"The job sucks. I've seen the way some of the men treat you. You shouldn't be working in a hotel."

"You're seriously talking to me about my job while we're in this situation? We've been kidnapped, and you're striking a deal about drugs. It sucks."

"I've got nothing else to do with my time."

"Why aren't you looking for a way out?" she asked, getting off the toilet and washing her hands.

"I've already checked, babe. The window is locked tight, and I imagine they've got men on the outside who're waiting for me to slip up." His words didn't fill her with any kind of comfort.

"So we're stuck here. Is Caleb even coming to get us?"

"Caleb and Elijah are coming. I wouldn't put you in danger." She made to flush the toilet, but he stopped her.

"I don't know you, and you don't know me."

"I know you enough, and what better time to distract you."

"Why did you call me a whore?"

"If you don't mean anything to me then they can't use you against me. A whore's a whore. There's nothing special about you other than the fact I like to fuck you."

"We've never—"

He pressed a finger against her lips. "They don't need to know that. I'm doing this to save you."

Nodding, she stared at her hands. She rubbed her palms together wishing for her nice warm bed, hot chocolate, and book. There was nothing more comforting than a good book to settle down to.

"Hey, I'm going to get us out of this."

"Everything hurts, Henry."

"Do you believe me?" he asked.

She shrugged. "I don't know what I believe anymore." The only hope she had of getting out of this alive was to trust him.

Henry cupped her cheek, gently. The bruise must look awful. She didn't know how bad she looked as there were no mirrors in the room.

"I'm not going to let anything bad happen to you, I promise." His fingers stroked a length down to her neck.

Her pulse raced at the smallest contact of his fingers. She licked her lips and stared into his eyes. There was no fear or panic in his depths, only lust shining back at her. Was it lust, or was she hoping to see something that wasn't actually there?

"I'm afraid."

"Good, being afraid is good." His gaze dropped to her lips.

She held her breath waiting for him to do something, anything.

A bang on the door interrupted their moment. "Hurry up in there."

Lydia withdrew from his touch, looking at Henry.

"You're going to have to get on your knees."

Chapter Three

The last thing Henry wanted to say to her in that moment was for her to get to her knees. Fuck, the next time he said shit like that to her, he wanted her to get to her knees because she wanted to. He was fucked in the head; there was no doubt about it. Opening the door, he glared at Bill but waited for Lydia to crawl out of the bathroom.

"You've got this whore trained well."

Throughout the whole of his life, Henry had never cared about women. They were useful for getting a rock off but nothing else. Lydia didn't deserve this, nor did she deserve any of the bruises on her body. She'd removed the stockings to show off her gorgeous pale legs. Every time she'd been in a skirt he'd wanted to run his hands up and down those pale thighs.

This kidnapping was driving him crazy. Lydia could do much better than him or Darren. Her last boyfriend had almost killed her, and now if Henry wasn't careful, he'd be the one to get her killed.

Caleb had known he'd been taken. In the background Henry had heard Donna's frantic voice. When Caleb had asked if Lydia was there, he'd confirmed with a hum.

His friend would come and bring Elijah with them.

"We can't take them out now, Henry. You're going to have to wait to kill them."

"Fine, but make sure it's quick." He hated not being able to talk openly. If it had just been him they'd taken, he'd have forced their hand. Lydia made him keep his tongue in check.

Standing out of the bathroom with Lydia in front of him, he felt exposed. "I think it's time she went downstairs."

"No, she's a whore, and I want some entertainment," Leon said, sitting down. "I don't know how long Caleb's going to take. How much does your bitch cost?"

She sat by his legs, but he felt her body shake.

"Sorry, boys, I don't share."

Bill and Leon shared a look. The men around them all looked to one another, smirking. They held guns. They were the ones in control.

"Seriously, she's used to having dick," Bill said.

"Not just any dick. Only mine." The lies were mounting up. He stared at all of them, remembering their faces for when he was going to tear them apart.

This was getting out of hand. He knew they were going to ask for a show, but he wasn't interested in giving one.

"I don't care what dick she picks. I want some action, or I'm going to start hurting her," Bill said.

"You hurt her and the deal is off with Caleb."

"I didn't realize this whore was so valuable." Leon spoke this time, tilting his head to the side.

"She's not valuable. I like to fuck her. She's not going to put on a show. I like them chunky. Not only that, hurt her, and you'll be the ones that will have to deal with Caleb and Elijah. She works for them. They'll have to replace her." He folded his arms, waiting for them to speak. Henry was trying to use any excuse to stop them from looking at her. Both men had mentioned her weight. Henry didn't mind her fuller, rounder figure, but they did.

"You're right. She's too fucking fat to watch her. Fuck this," Leon said, standing up.

Time passed, he didn't know how much, until Bill got to his feet, being the one to make the final decision. From the look in Bill's eye, Henry sensed he wanted her but wasn't going to let the others know he wanted her. "Time for you both to be put back in the basement."

Before Henry could move, Bill grabbed Lydia's hair and dragged her to her feet. She screamed, crying out.

Henry went to stop Bill, but two men held him back. He was angry they'd gotten around him, pissed off that they were hurting her. Each man was going to die slowly, painfully, and all of the deaths were going to be at his hands.

Bill grabbed her face, applying pressure to her jaw. The pain showed on her face. Henry fought the men that held him.

"If I didn't want this deal so bad you'd be bent over taking my cock in that pussy of yours. Once I was done, I'd give you to my men to play with, if they could get past their revulsion of your fat ass." Bill grabbed her ass, pulling her in close. Henry had underestimated Bill.

"You leave her the fuck alone." Henry snarled the words, wanting them to leave Lydia alone. Nothing could happen to her; he wouldn't let it.

"Until I get what I want, you're safe." Bill threw her off him, and she landed against the pool table, crying out as she collapsed to the floor.

Fighting with all of his might, Henry was led back downstairs as Lydia, in pain, was forced to crawl. He didn't like this one bit, and when he finally got the chance all of the men were going to die.

They chained him to the bed and Lydia as well, leaving one of their hands free. He didn't know why they did that, but he wasn't interested. They were a shit operation that had caught him unawares. He was angry at himself for putting them both in this situation. If he'd not chased her down the fucking street, he might not be considering mass murder.

"Are you all right?" he asked once they were alone again.

His heart was hammering against his chest. He was so angry and helpless at the same time. Any other time he'd have killed them with ease and not cared about the damage done to him, but he had Lydia to consider.

"I'm fine."

"No, you're not. You're holding your side where you hit the pool table. You're clearly not all right."

She blew out a breath, and he looked toward her.

"I'll be fine. There's nothing you can do. It just really hurts."

"I'm so sorry about this."

"It's okay. Thank you for not, erm, you know, making me do anything out there."

"I won't let them touch you, Lydia." He shuffled on the bed to get closer to her. Pressing his body against her side, he did everything he could to help her feel warm.

"I'm really sorry about this," she said.

"No, you don't get to apologize." He wanted to hold her in his arms, to do anything that would help her. Instead, he tried to give her warmth and doing a shit job at it.

"Talk to me about something else." She rested her head against his shoulder.

"Like what?"

"I don't know, tell me something that no one knows about you." She let out a sigh.

"You tell me first. I've never done this before."

"What? Had a conversation with a woman?"

Henry rested his head against hers. "No, I've not had a conversation with a woman before. I usually ask her how much she'll cost and then pay her. We fuck or she sucks me off. I pay her, and then I leave." Thinking back over the last few years he couldn't recall a single conversation with a woman other than Lydia.

"What about Donna? You must have spoken to her."

"There's nothing I can say that will make her feel comfortable. I'd more than likely scare her." Caleb had asked for him to be nice to Donna. If he couldn't say anything nice then don't say anything at all. For the most part, he kept his mouth shut around his friend's woman.

"Wow, okay then. Erm, I don't like boiled eggs. I find them disgusting."

"Boiled eggs?"

"Yeah, I know. I think they're supposed to be healthy for you, but I can't stand to have my eggs boiled. It's gross, and then when people split them down and add more crap to them? Yuck, no thanks."

He chuckled. "I don't really care for food so long as I'm not starving."

"I love food. I love cooking and eating, but I try not to do too much."

"Why?"

"I've got no one to share it with. Nothing sucks more than making food only to realize you've got to throw it in the trash."

"I'm sorry to hear about that."

"Me, too. I hate being alone." She sounded so lost. He didn't want her to feel lost.

"I hate paying whores for favors," he said, blurting out the truth.

She pulled away, looking at him. "What?"

"In the beginning I thought it was fun. I didn't have to worry about finding women to fuck, but over the years, it's gotten a little old." He didn't know why he was telling her the truth.

"Why don't you stop? Find a real woman?" She tilted her head back to look at him.

He smiled, not feeling any real need to smile. "This is a lot easier than trying to get a woman to see past the scars and the job."

"Your scars are not that bad."

"They are. You'd be surprised how many women can't stand to have a man who's less than perfect."

"Be careful, Henry, you're going to show your feminine side."

He chuckled. "Is that a bad thing with you?"

"Not with me. I won't tell anyone, I promise."

Closing his eyes, he inhaled her lavender scent and wished there was something he could do to take the pain away from her.

"I never loved Darren," she said, seconds later.

"You didn't?"

"No. I was pissed when he held me as a shield. The prick, I hated him."

He didn't say anything else. Darren was an asshole who couldn't keep shit to himself.

"I never thanked you for saving me."

Henry stared down into her brown gaze. "You don't need to thank me."

"If you hadn't been there or done what you did, I'd be dead."

"You're thanking me for making your apartment a mess?"

She shook her head. "I'm thanking you for not walking away."

"I won't walk away, and I won't leave you here either, Lydia."

****

Resting her head against Henry's shoulder, she closed her eyes finally relaxing. She believed everything he said. Henry didn't strike her as the kind of man to go back on his word. So far he'd been with her the whole time.

"We'll be gone soon."

"Good. I smell, and I'm desperate need of a shower." She was in a lot of pain. Hitting the pool table hadn't been a lot of fun. "Why would you make a deal with these bastards?"

"Caleb deals with the business." He leaned in close so his lips were by her ear. "I'll kill every last one of these bastards in time, Lydia. You've just got to trust me."

"I will." She didn't mind him killing these men. They were horrid and had caused her a lot of pain.

Time passed, and every now and again Henry would try to talk to her. She listened to him, finding him interesting, which surprised her. When he'd admitted the truth about the whores, she'd seen a part of him she doubted he let anyone see.

The scars on his face didn't bother her. Sure, when she first met him she'd been scared, but she also had the information Darren told her. Henry hadn't done anything to hurt her, apart from his awful words earlier in the night.

God, she was starting to like him, and it was impossible for her to like him.

She tensed as she heard the door being unlocked and Bill appeared. Behind him stood Caleb and a man she didn't recognize.

"It's your lucky day. We've made a deal, and now you can both leave," Bill said.

"I see you weren't particularly good at taking my man?" Caleb asked. He wore a suit and looked entirely collected.

Henry was released, but he didn't move away from her. She lifted her head from his shoulder.

"Release her," Henry said.

"The deal was for you, not her."

"Bill, I didn't make a deal to cause problems. Release Henry and his woman, or I swear to you, you won't make it out of this room alive," Caleb said.

Whoever these men were they didn't know when to shut up. She didn't want to be left alone.

"Fine." Bill tugged at her hand making her gasp at the sudden pain.

"Hey, fucking watch it," Henry said.

She was thrust against Henry.

"Get out. We'll talk more," Bill said, following behind them as they were taken upstairs. She buried her face against Henry's chest liking his arms wrapped around her.

The warm air hit her face, and she was led toward a large car. Climbing in the back, Henry climbed in beside her. Caleb and the other man joined them. The man she didn't know hit the window to the front. "Start driving."

"What the fuck happened?" Caleb asked.

Henry didn't release her. "We started arguing, and I was an asshole. We were on the street, and I didn't think about where we were. They drove up and took us. I'm sorry, Caleb. I fucked up."

"Lydia, are you all right?" Caleb asked.

"Yeah, I'm fine."

"Should we be talking with this whore in the car?" the mystery man asked.

"She's not a fucking whore," Henry said, yelling.

"Elijah, this is Lydia. She's Donna's friend."

The man looked at her and nodded. "I apologize. I wasn't given all the information. I wouldn't have called you a whore if I knew."

"It's okay."

"She needs to see a doctor. They were not gentle with her." Henry told them about her hitting the brick wall then the pool table. "She might have broken a rib or something."

"We're going back to my house," Caleb said. "Donna's worried about you, Lydia. She wants to make sure you're okay. You're also not staying alone for the time being. I didn't like the way Bill was looking at you."

"I want to go home," she said. All she wanted was to curl up in her bed and cry. She didn't want these men to witness her breaking down.

"No, you're not going home. I saw the way Bill was looking at you," Henry said. "I'm going to stay at Caleb's tonight. You're not leaving."

"Okay, I won't leave." She wasn't in the mood to start arguing with him.

"Who are they?" Henry asked.

Their voices drowned out as she stared out of the window. She didn't want to hear anything about who the men were. In fact, all she wanted to do was forget they'd been in her life.

The three continued to talk, and she watched the sun coming up. Had they really been gone all night?

"What day is it?" she asked, glancing back at the three men.

"It's Sunday morning, Lydia." Caleb answered her.

"Has it really been that long?" She didn't realize the time was passing so much. They hadn't fed them or given them water. No wonder she was tired. She'd been too scared to simply fall asleep.

"Yeah, it's how Donna found out you were gone. I'm really sorry this happened to you."

"Yeah, me, too." She went back to looking out of the window.

She recognized Caleb's country home with the security fence. The car came to a stop, and Caleb pulled out his cell phone. "Hey, baby, we're here. Would you open the gate?"

The metal gates started to open.

"Why didn't you use the code?" Henry asked.

"I didn't want Donna worrying in case someone got in. I told her I'd call when we had you to take care of opening the gate. She didn't want to fall asleep."

"You've found yourself a keeper," Elijah said.

Donna was one of those women that men adored. Her full figure didn't detract from her beauty. They saw the true beauty in her eyes.

"I know. Keep your hands and eyes off my woman. Donna's mine. Find your own woman." Caleb sent out a warning.

Lydia smiled.

Glancing behind her, she saw the gates slide closed. Seeing the rest of the world closed out, she finally felt safe.

Donna stood at the door waiting for them. Luke was on her hip as she looked out toward them.

Caleb climbed out of the car first. "Get back inside the house." He didn't stay with them.

"What? I want to see Lydia."

"He's very protective of her," Henry said.

"I can see that."

Lydia stood between Elijah and Henry as they made their way into Caleb's house.

"I had to feed him, and there's no point me being alone. I was only waiting by the door."

"It's dangerous for you, baby. You can't just do that. What if I'd been taken and I was being forced to get inside the house?"

Lydia listened to him argue with Donna.

"I know that's never going to happen."

"How?" Caleb asked.

"Because you wouldn't have brought anyone to the house. You've have taken them to your penthouse or somewhere else. You're not stupid, Caleb." She watched as Donna went on her toes and kissed him. "I love you for caring."

Donna turned and finally saw her. Lydia listened as she gasped. "Are you okay?" Within seconds Donna and the baby were in front of her.

"I'm fine, seriously."

"She's going to be checked over by a doctor," Henry said, speaking over her.

"Come on. I made up one of the bedrooms for you. I also made another one up for you, Henry, if you'd like to stay." Donna didn't wait around. "Send the doctor up as soon as he arrives."

Lydia glanced behind her to look at Henry. He offered her a smile, and that was all.

Following Donna upstairs, Lydia saw the bedroom was near to hers.

"You don't need to put me so close. I'm a big girl," Lydia said.

"From the look of your face you've been through hell. I'm not having you anywhere else right now. Don't worry, Henry's near you as well. He looks awful."

"It has been an awful night. Believe me, I don't want to remember it." Lydia stared at the white sheet on the bed and decided against sitting there.

"Come on, the bathroom's through here. Caleb wanted there to be an en suite in every bedroom." Donna opened the second door inside the room to reveal a luxury bathroom.

"Wow, he really didn't spare any expense."

"I'll give you some privacy. I need to finish feeding Luke. I'm so pleased you're okay. We'll talk soon."

Donna was gone out of the door before she could say anything. Blowing out a breath, Lydia looked around at the luxury her friend lived in. Caleb's love could never be questioned.

Stepping toward the mirror, she winced as she caught sight of her reflection. The left side of her face was badly bruised. Lifting up her dress, she saw there were also bruises over her body. The side where she'd connected with the pool table hurt the most.

It's okay, Lydia, you're safe now.

She turned the water on, and she watched the tub fill up.

Tucking hair behind her ear, she thought about Henry. Her feelings about the brutish man scared her more than anything. He could have left her there to be used, abused, and killed. He hadn't. Why?

There was more to Henry than she first thought, and being intrigued by a man who was deadly terrified her.

Chapter Four

"That woman is going to be the death of me, I'm sure of it," Caleb said, turning toward them. "Let's talk in my office."

When Lydia was out of sight, Henry followed his friend, closing the door behind him. He didn't like not knowing where Lydia was. She'd been so scared during their time together. Seeing her in the large house with the lights shining around them, she'd looked broken.

"What did you have to agree to?" Henry asked, still pissed at himself for putting them all in this position. He shouldn't have upset Lydia, sending her running, nor should he have gone after her.

"We're expanding a venture into rural towns along with accepting them as our suppliers for the future." Caleb sat down behind his desk while Elijah took the sofa.

"I'm pissed off," Elijah said. "I've got a good deal going with the Mexicans. I don't want to risk my ass because of some two bit townies."

"They're not townies, Elijah. I told you that. Bill and Leon are front men. They're not the men running the show. Someone else is."

"Drake Stone? He wouldn't use those guys. They're next to useless," Henry said. Drake was their enemy and tried to fight for the right to run the whole city. They were all powerful men, but Drake was an asshole of the highest order. He got women hooked on drugs, then put the addicts on the books. His operation was sloppy and violent. Henry loved violence, but with him getting older he was seeing the need to keep his fists firmly in his pockets.

"It could be Drake."

"That little shit would be bragging about having him," Elijah said, pointing at Henry. "He's nothing better than a twelve-year-old with a gun. Drake couldn't keep quiet to save his own ass let alone anyone else. It can't be Drake."

"Why not? We know him as being a pain in the ass little shit. This is a competition to him. How do we know he's not about to take on something else? Let's face it, he knew we'd rule this out," Caleb said. "I'm not going to rule him out, not yet."

"When can I kill them?" Henry asked, more interested in hurting the men who'd hurt Lydia.

"You can't kill them yet. We need to find out what else they know before we take them out."

"No, I'm the one who's going to be taking them out, no one else." Henry wanted their blood on his hands to know he did the job right.

"Are you okay?" Caleb asked.

"I'm fine. This isn't the first time I've been taken, and I imagine it's not going to be the last. Don't worry about me."

He stood up and started to pace the room. Glancing at the clock on the wall he saw it was a little after seven.

"Lydia can't be alone," Elijah said, speaking up.

"What?" Henry paused to look at the other man.

"We don't know if they're going to be watching her. Bill didn't look all that stable," Caleb said.

"And yet you struck a deal."

"It was either strike a deal with them or put you and Lydia at risk. From the crazed look on your face I imagine you wouldn't want me to put her in a situation that will change her."

Caleb's knowing words irritated him.

"I've not got to listen to this." Walking toward the door, Henry was ready to leave.

"They're going to come back. If this isn't Drake then it's going to be someone else. You can't let her be alone."

"Don't worry. I'll be on babysitting duty." Henry opened the door, walking away.

He needed a drink, and it was too early to get started on alcohol. Stepping into the kitchen he came to a stop as he saw Donna sitting at the table. A cloth was over her shoulder, but the sight of Luke's legs let Henry know what she was doing.

"Where's Lydia?" he asked, going to the coffee pot. He saw it was still brewing and cursed.

"She's taking a shower. I want to thank you for taking care of her. When we realized she'd been taken, we were both so worried."

He glanced over his shoulder to see Donna looking at him.

"Sure, no problem. The doctor should be here soon."

"I know. I'm letting this guy have his feed and then I'm going to get some food ready for Lydia. Did you guys eat?" Donna asked.

"We were kidnapped. What do you think?" He snapped at her, angry that she'd ask such a stupid question.

"Henry, a word," Caleb said, drawing him toward the entrance of the kitchen.

Fuck.

He followed his friend. "I'm sorry."

"I don't tell Donna everything that goes on. She knows you were taken, but you don't need to take out your anger on her. This is not her fault, far from it. I'm the one to blame."

"I'm sorry." Henry repeated his apology. "I'm hungry, tired, and fucked off."

"Sorry, Donna. It has been a long night. I shouldn't have snapped at you like that," Henry said, apologizing.

"It's okay. I can't imagine what you're going through." She was rubbing Luke's back as she spoke.

"I'm going to set up some food for Lydia and I'll get out of your way." He pulled out several different meats and cheese from the fridge. Arranging two plates of food, he poured coffee into cups, and asked where Lydia was sleeping.

"I put her in the room next to mine and Caleb's. You're next door to her."

He didn't stay around to talk.

Elijah was nowhere to be seen, but Henry wasn't interested in work. He needed to see Lydia before he completely lost his shit. The doctor still hadn't arrived. Knocking on the door, he waited for Lydia to answer the door.

Seconds passed before she opened the door. She wore a thick white robe with a towel wrapped around her head.

"Hey," he said, not knowing what to say. He truly was used to women paid to be in his company. Those women didn't need kind words or understanding, just money.

"Is that for me?" She stared at the plate, licking her lips.

"It certainly is." He held it up. "Can I join you? I'm not really good company for anyone else."

"Sure." She stepped back letting him inside her room. The scent of lavender was heavy in the room. He was becoming addicted to the smell.

Lydia took gentle steps to the bed and climbed on the covers. He waited for her to be settled before placing the tray on her legs. Sitting in front of her, he rested the tray on his knee.

"You're still dirty," she said.

"I've not had time to shower. I needed to get up to speed with what Caleb had to agree to."

"Will you be going into business with them?" He saw her shudder.

"No, we won't be going into business with them. I made you a promise, Lydia, and I'm going to stick with it."

She stared at him. Her dark brown gaze focused on him. "Good." He barely caught what she said as she whispered it.

Nodding, he took a sip of his coffee, watching her eat the meat and fruit. She didn't pull any faces of disgust at what he'd given to her.

"I'm going to sleep here tonight, and then I'm going to head home," she said.

Picking up a piece of boiled ham he started to eat the meat. "You can't go back home, Lydia."

"What do you mean? You had an agreement with them. They wouldn't be coming after me, would they?" The fear flashed on her face.

"They believe you're my whore. I didn't know what was going on, but if they thought you meant anything to me they would have used you against me."

"I don't mean anything to you."

"This was where I struggled with the decision. If they believed you didn't mean anything they might have taken you regardless. I was trying to save you. I can't have your death on my conscience." He had blood on his hands, the blood of men who deserved it. Lydia was different, and he'd known it the first time he spotted her in the jewelry store. Caleb had been talking with the blonde, and Henry had not been able to look away from Lydia. He tried to stay away. Then when Caleb gave him the order to get rid of Darren, he'd found himself in her life once again. The last thing he wanted to do was hurt her, yet it seemed all he was good for was hurting her.

"I know what you were trying to do. It's hard to believe, but I did understand. A lot of men keep calling me a whore. It's getting a little tiring." She rubbed at her temple, wincing as she jolted her body.

"Are you hurt?" He put his plate on the bed beside him. Henry took her plate from her and tugged her to her feet. "Don't try to lie to me. I want the truth."

She stood up.

"Show me where it hurts?"

"I'm naked."

"I've seen a lot of women naked. I won't say anything. Just show me where you're hurt." If she was in too much pain he wasn't going to sit around waiting for the doctor.

Lydia tugged at the belt tying the robe together. She turned her back on him and loosened the robe before turning back to him.

He saw the top part of her chest.

"Where does it hurt?" His cock was hardening as more of her body was revealed to his gaze.

"My right side."

Henry reached out to open the robe. She dropped her hand to stop him.

"I've got to see you." He stared up into her eyes. Tears filled her depths.

"Okay." She released his hand, averting her gaze as he slid the robe open.

It took every ounce of strength not to look at her pussy. He saw the dark bruising across her ribs. Henry didn't have a clue what he was looking for. All he saw was the bruising, but at least none of her ribs were poking through her skin. *They could be poking organs inside her body.* He wasn't going to worry her.

"I don't think they're broken. You might have cracked one or two." That seemed the more logical explanation.

His mouth ran dry. Could he smell her pussy?

Standing up, he gave her space to cover her body.

He didn't want her to cover up. Reaching out, he stopped her. She stared at him, and he closed the distance between them. Lydia tilted her head back to look in his eyes. He didn't see the bruise on the side of her face, or the pain in her eyes. Henry saw the woman he'd seem many times but kept himself away from.

Cupping her cheek, he stroked a thumb across her lips. "I'm going to make each of them pay."

She did something that shocked him. Lydia licked the tip of his thumb. "Thank you."

He leaned down, wanting to know what those plump lips tasted like.

The door opening stopped him. He withdrew his hand and took a step back.

"The doctor's here," Donna said.

Lydia put her robe back into place.

"I'll give you some privacy. I need to clean up." He picked up his plate and coffee, leaving the room without another glance behind him.

He needed a shower and to get some focus on his troubled thoughts.

****

Lydia ignored Donna's obvious stare. The doctor pressed on her ribs. He was a middle aged man with greying hair. His hands were cold, though, and it was distracting her from the pain.

"You're very lucky. Two cracked ribs and a lot of bruising."

"That's lucky?" she asked, wrapping the robe around her once he bound up her ribs.

"I've seen a lot worse. I heard what happened. Believe me, Henry saved your ass from a lot more pain." He took a step back, writing something down on a notebook. "You're going to be in a lot of pain, but you're going to need to rest for a couple of weeks."

"I don't have the time to rest. I need to be working." She didn't want to lose her job at the hotel chain. It was boring, but it paid the bills and kept her above water.

"I'm sorry. You're not going to get well unless you listen to me, and that means resting. You can argue with me all you want. If you don't rest then you're going to end up being off work for a lot longer than a couple of weeks." The doctor packed his kit away.

"I'll make sure she rests, doctor," Donna said, glaring at her.

"Make sure she does. I'm going to see Caleb." He gave her another look then turned to leave.

"You've got to rest, Lydia." Donna started listing all the things that could go wrong if she didn't rest.

Rubbing at her temples, she looked at her friend.

"I will, Donna. Not all of us have a rich man to live off." Her words were harsh, and she regretted them the moment she said them. "Fuck, forget I said anything."

"You think I'm living off Caleb?"

"No, I don't think that. You're both in love. Look, it has been a long couple of days. I'm in pain, and I'm tired. My mouth is running away with me." Getting to her feet, she pulled the other woman in for a hug. She loved Donna like a sister. Even though they no longer worked together they'd grown close, and Lydia didn't want to lose her friend. If she kept talking shit to her, she knew Caleb would be seriously pissed at her.

"Okay, so are you going to tell me what's going on between you and Henry?"

Lydia groaned. "Nothing is going on between us. We went through something together, and he saved me."

She wasn't going to think any more about what happened. Henry had saved her from a lot more pain.

Pushing hair off her face, she winced as the sudden movement jolted her body.

"I'm going to leave you to get some rest. I'll see you soon."

Glancing at the clock, Lydia saw it was past nine. She watched Donna grab the plate and cup then leave the room.

Once the door closed, she walked over to the bed and sat down. Staring at her feet she wondered what was going to happen to her in the next couple of days. For most of her life she'd stayed out of the way, not getting into any kind of trouble. One mistaken night out and she was in a lot of trouble.

Lying down on top of the blanket she stared at the plain white ceiling. She'd thought sleep would come to her easily, but it was actually being a pain in the ass.

Getting to her feet, she opened her door to find silence met her ears. She hadn't heard Donna or Caleb leave. The house was big enough to hide in.

She stepped down to the bedroom next to hers. Knocking on the door, she waited. Rubbing her hands together she wondered if he was still asleep. When seconds passed and he still hadn't answered the door, she started to walk back to her room.

"What's up?" Henry asked, opening the door.

"I can't sleep."

His hair was wet.

"Did I get you out of the shower?" she asked.

"Yeah, I smell and need a wash." There was a towel around his hips. "Come on in." She brushed past him to see his room was very much like hers.

"You make yourself at home?"

"Caleb's like a brother to me. We're business partners, and I hope he'd do the same when I get a place of my own."

"You don't have a place?"

"I do, but I never actually go there. I tend to crash at Caleb's place." He closed the door, flicking the lock into place.

She wasn't scared to hear the sound. For once she wanted to shut the rest of the world out, but she didn't want to be alone either.

"Make yourself comfortable. I'll finish up." He didn't close the bathroom door all the way. She listened to the sound of shower as she lay down in his bed.

Time passed, and soon the shower stopped running. She watched the door, and he appeared wearing a pair of sweat pants but no shirt. The bruises and more scars stood out on his body. The light in the bedroom was on for her to see.

"You're staring," he said.

He walked over to the bed, climbing under the covers.

She didn't say anything or tense up as he slid into bed beside her. Lydia still wore the robe as she'd not found any clothes and had forgotten to ask Donna for some.

"Thank you."

"For what?"

"Saving me. The doctor said it could have gone a lot worse if you didn't do what you did. I really appreciate everything you've done to help me." She tucked some hair behind her ear.

"What did the doctor say?"

She told him that she had cracked a couple of ribs but most of her pain was down to bruises. "I've got to rest."

"Then you better do what the doctor said," he said, stroking her cheek.

"I can't, Henry. I need to go to work or I won't be able to pay my bills."

"You need to stop thinking about the bills and think about your health. Your ribs could get worse." He removed his hand, laying her palm flat on the pillow between them. "I'll take care of you."

She stared at him, wishing her heart didn't race a little faster or her body melt a little harder at his closeness. This was the first time she'd been this close to him without them being strapped to a bed.

His eyes were a startling green. There was a coldness inside him, and yet she saw something else, something deeper.

"You're not going to argue with me?" he asked.

"I want to, but I'm in too much pain to think of a good argument." She smiled, blowing out a sigh.

"You'll be back to fighting me in no time."

"Will I ever be normal again?" she asked, feeling a tad broken. She'd never needed to sleep beside a man to feel safe before.

"In a couple of weeks, maybe longer. Before you know what happens you've forgotten everything you've been through and you're living life."

She nodded, staring past his shoulder. "And you're going to kill them all?"

"Yes, not tonight, not tomorrow, probably not next week, but I'm going to kill them."

"I want you to kill them." Tears filled her eyes, and she returned her gaze to him. "Does that make me a bad person?"

"The last person you need to ask that is me. I don't give a fuck what happens to them. They hurt you, and they're going to die."

She grabbed his hand and locked their fingers together.

"You're going to go to sleep now, Lydia. Nothing is going to happen to you. Caleb's home, and I'm here."

"Why do I feel happier and safer knowing that you're here?"

Henry smiled. "I hope it's because of my dazzling personality."

She laughed at his teasing.

"Go to sleep, Lydia. Everything will be okay. The bad guys are not going to hurt you. I'm going to take care of you."

She closed her eyes as his breath fanned across her face. Every now and then she opened her eyes to see Henry staring back at her. "Trust me, baby."

"I trust you." She closed her eyes and tucked his hand between her breasts, holding onto him.

Slowly, she started to relax. Henry's even breathing along with the masculine scent soothed her enough to finally fall asleep.

Chapter Five

"I don't think this is right," Lydia said.

Henry stood in the corner of Caleb's office while his friend told her what was going to happen. They'd spent the night together in his bed, and he didn't know what to say to her. She was the first woman to be in his bed, and he didn't even need to leave a payment as no services had passed between them.

She wore one of Donna's maternity shirts and drawstring pants. The clothing swamped her and looked completely out of place. She looked maternal in the clothes even though there was no baby.

"You're Donna's best friend. I can't let anything happen to you, and this is our fault that we've brought you into this. After Darren, I hoped not to draw you into any of our shit, but it happened and I can't apologize enough."

Lydia held her hand up. "I don't care. It wasn't something we knew was going to happen." She looked behind her at him. "We made a mistake arguing like we did."

"I know, but you've got to listen to him. I'm going to be the one to take care of you, Lydia. After what happened the last couple of days I don't want you alone." If any of the bastards started sniffing around Lydia, Henry wanted to be around to kill them. No one was going to help him take the men out. Henry wanted that privilege all to himself.

"If you're happy to be with me then I'll agree to it. I don't want Donna worried either." Lydia turned back to look at Caleb. "Thank you for responding quickly."

"Henry can be a total bastard and piss me off, but I wouldn't let anything happen to him either."

Caleb stood as Donna entered carrying Luke.

"What's going on?" she asked.

"I'm going to take Lydia home so she can rest. I'll deal with her job and take care of her." Henry stood away from the wall, offering his hand to Lydia. He noticed this morning that she moved a lot slower than normal.

She joined him, smiling at Donna.

"Oh, you don't have to leave immediately."

"Yeah, I do, Donna. If I don't go home now I never will." Lydia pulled Donna in for a hug. "I'll keep in touch, I promise."

Henry moved toward Caleb. "I need to borrow the car."

Caleb was already passing him the keys before he finished talking. "Take care and try not to find trouble or hurt Lydia. I don't want to have to deal with Donna being pissed."

Donna was rarely pissed with Caleb.

Taking the keys, Henry broke up the women's hug and helped walk Lydia down to the car.

Both of their friends stood at the entrance waiting for them to leave. He secured Lydia into the car then moved toward the passenger side. Giving Caleb a wave, he got behind the wheel and started the car up.

"Would you take it slowly? Donna squeezed me a little too tightly."

He took the drive slowly, easing out of the gates and taking off into the city. Henry missed the potholes in the road, making sure to go easy.

"Why didn't you scream or yell or something?" he asked, annoyed that Donna hadn't hugged her easily.

"I don't know." She tugged at the bottom of the shirt. "God, I can't believe I'm wearing these."

"They're cute."

"I've no intention of being a mother. Donna's sweet. Motherhood suits her, but God, these are a nightmare."

He laughed at the disdain in her voice.

"You better not tell her I said that."

"Don't worry. I won't. If I said anything awful to Donna, Caleb would kick my ass and be happy while he did it."

"She's a lovely friend but doesn't have the best taste in clothing." Lydia sighed, running her hand down her legs.

"If it makes you feel any better, I think you look cute."

He looked toward her, seeing her cheeks heat under his compliment. "Are you blushing?"

"A little. I don't know how to take you right now." She pushed her hair behind her.

"What do you mean?"

"You've never been the nicest man to get to know. I don't know. You're coming across as being kind of sweet."

He gasped, turning to look at her. "Don't ever tell anyone that I'm being sweet."

"Are you going to stop visiting your whores?" she asked, changing the subject.

"Jesus, woman, you're going to give me fucking whiplash with the change of conversation."

"Answer the question."

Henry pulled into the parking lot for her apartment. The rest of the cars were not as classy as Caleb's. Cutting the engine, he glanced over at her. She was resting against the door, staring at him.

"I don't know. Why do you ask?"

"Last night you said that you hated going to whores. I just wondered if you were going to make a change or stick to doing what you clearly like doing."

Was she jealous?

"I don't know what I'm going to do. I've not found a woman to look past the scars. I've got needs, and for a price whores fill them."

Tears were shining in her eyes. "It's, erm, it's good to know."

She scrambled out of the car, confusing him more.

Following behind her, it didn't take him long to keep into step beside her.

Her movements were slow as she was still in pain. He didn't rush her.

"What's with the attitude?" he asked, opening the door for her to go through.

"Nothing is wrong. I've not got an attitude."

They walked toward the elevator only to see that it was out of order.

Lydia cursed. "Great, this is not my day." She pressed a hand to her head.

What was he missing?

They walked toward the steps, and he made sure to stand behind her. She lived on the fifth floor. He'd be having a word with maintenance and the landlord in the next couple of hours. By the time they made it up the first flight of stairs, she stopped, pressing a hand to her ribs.

"I'm sorry," she said.

"Don't worry. Take your time."

"How are you doing it?" She leaned against the wall and looked at him through hooded eyes.

"What?"

"Not hurting."

He smiled. "I'm not the one with the cracked ribs. Come on, you can lean on me." He wrapped an arm around her waist and pulled her close to him. Henry was careful not to jar her body or cause her any more pain.

"Thank you," she said, taking the steps slowly.

"No problem."

Together they made their way up to her apartment. Nothing had changed since the last time he came here. He had the keys and eased them into the lock, opening the door with ease.

"I don't like how little you take care of yourself. There should be a lot more security here for a woman living alone."

"I rarely cause problems, Henry. The only problem I see is the fact I hang around with a woman who has criminals for friends."

"We're not all bad criminals." He locked the door, looking at the flimsy piece of metal keeping other people away. "This is not going to do at all."

"What do you mean? I've never had any problems before. This is my place, and I've never had any problems with it." She lowered herself onto her ratty sofa.

Her space was small yet filled with so much personality. It was vibrant, like the woman. He was shocked by how feminine her space had become since he last visited. The last time he visited being when he killed her then-boyfriend. It was not a good idea to bring that up. Staring at the lock he knew he needed to take their safety in his own hands.

"We're not staying here." He moved from the sitting room and opened the first door across the room. He found the bathroom, and the door next to that was a store room.

The only door left led him straight to her bedroom.

Pulling out his cell phone he dialed Caleb's number.

"You've only just gone. Are you having trouble already?"

"No. Change of plans. There's no way she and I can stay here. It's unsafe, and there's no way I'm not sleeping just to keep us alive." He opened doors to her wardrobe finding a suitcase. "I'm going to take her to my condo."

"Seriously? Is there something going on that I don't know about?"

Henry paused. There was nothing going on between them even though every time he saw her all he wanted to do was kiss her. "No, nothing is going on. I'm trying to keep her safe. She doesn't deserve to be hurt."

Glancing at the door, he saw her watching him. Her lips were formed in a perfect O as she stared from him to the bed.

"I've got to go. If you need me I'll be at the condo. Find out everything you can from Drake."

"You're not hiding, are you?"

"I'm not hiding, but I'm not leaving her alone for the next couple of weeks. It's what the doctor said for her. You wouldn't want Donna to be pissed at you."

"No. Fine, I'll let Donna know that you're taking care of her friend. Nothing better not happen to her or I swear it will be you dealing with my wife."

"Unlike you, Donna doesn't scare me." He hung up the phone and started going through her wardrobe, grabbing sweat pants and shirts.

"What are you doing?" She stayed by the door watching him.

"You need rest so you're all better. If it wasn't for me being a total bastard to you, we wouldn't be in this situation. We're going to my place. It's a condo within the center of the city. It's nice and quiet. We won't be disturbed there."

"What's wrong with my place?"

"You've got a tiny lock that I could take down with one kick. Anyone can get to us and I don't trust the new business deal we've set up with Bill and Leon." He threw underwear into the suitcase then looked at her women's perfumes. Scooping them up, he placed them on the suitcase as well.

"We're leaving right away. I suggest you grab anything you want. We're leaving."

She didn't put up a fight and moved past him to kneel on the floor. He watched her ass thrust up in the air as she delved under the bed and pulled out a shoebox. His curiosity got the better of him. He looked over her shoulder in time to see the gun glinting up at him.

"What the fuck did you get a gun for?" he asked, taking a step back as she picked it up.

"After Darren, I got scared. I don't want to die. I've been practicing how to shoot."

Henry stepped out of her way as she pointed it off in another direction.

"Fuck. Baby, put that gun away. You're going to shoot my dick off if we're not careful." He stepped closer, extracting the gun from her fingers. "Right, I'm going to have that." He checked the gun and swore as he saw there was no safety on. She'd been storing a gun with no safety on. "This isn't worth thinking about."

"You better give me my gun back."

"I'll give you the gun back when I think you're good enough to fucking shoot. Until then, you're not getting it and I'm not going to stand here and argue about this."

Once the safety was on, he slid the metal into the back of his jeans. "Let's go."

****

They were in the car again, and she didn't even have her gun. Lydia placed a palm over her side that hurt. The doctor had bound her ribs up tight so she could only just move.

"I can't believe you got a gun. If you were so scared why didn't you say anything to Donna?"

Resting her head on her hand, she stared at the man who was turning her entire world upside down. On the outside he was this scarred man with a rude attitude that pissed her off. Within a weekend he'd become something else, someone else. She saw a side of him that she didn't even think he was capable of possessing.

"Why are you staring at me like that?" he asked.

"You're always worried about something."

"Tell me. I want to know. Has someone been threatening you?"

She saw he gripped the steering wheel tightly. Letting out a sigh, she glanced out of the window. "Nothing and no one has been threatening me. For a long time after Darren, erm, I went a little crazy when you tried to warn him. I had a lot of nightmares about what happened."

"You've never talked about it?"

"No, not even with Donna. Caleb, he's very … protective of her. He wouldn't let me near her until he knew I wouldn't hurt her." She rubbed her nose recalling the fear that filled her when Caleb came to visit her. "It was strange being used as a shield. You saved me when you didn't have to. It would have probably been easier to kill me."

"I was following orders. Caleb didn't want me to kill you. He only wanted Darren to be given a warning. It was just luck that he'd fucked with enough people. I'm sorry you had to witness what happened." His grip didn't loosen from the steering wheel.

"Either way, you were very soothing to me during that day, which is strange. You helped me a lot."

"I helped clean up the mess. I didn't do anything else." He stopped at traffic lights and turned to look at her. "Are you okay?"

"I'm fine. I will be fine when everything gets cleared up and we don't have to worry about anything." She stared out of the window for the rest of the journey.

What else could she say to him?

He dealt with the traffic while she kept thinking about life. She needed to phone the hotel to let them know she wasn't going to come in. The moment she made that call she was going to be unemployed.

The time passed, and he put some music on the radio. She hummed to some of the tunes that she knew.

By the time he pulled up outside of a building she'd never seen before she was starving. The building looked like a new one and was surrounded by a steel gate. There were a couple more cars parked within the facility.

"Is this where you live?" she asked.

"Yeah." He climbed out of the car and moved to her side. She watched him open the door then reached out to grab her waist. His hands were so large as he helped her down from the vehicle. When she was around Henry, he made her feel small by how big he was.

Slowly, he lowered her to the floor as if she didn't weigh a thing.

He grabbed her suitcase, and together they made their way into the building. On the outside next to a wall she watched him press a card inside then type in a number.

"Are we entering a bank or something?" she asked.

"Nah, this is just a really secure building."

A man sat at the reception desk.

Staying by Henry's side, she followed him to the lift. The sterile, clinical feel of the building unnerved her.

"Is this where Caleb lives?"

"No. We both had an apartment in one of the blocks over there." He pointed to one of the tall building that didn't look too far as they travelled up the glass elevator, but she imagined was far enough to walk. "This is where I go when I want to relax, get away from everything."

"How long has it been since you came here last?" she asked.

"A couple of years. The building has a cleaning service that makes sure nothing is wrong with the place."

"Why has it been so long since you came here last?" She was curious about him. When she'd first met him, he had come across as a brutish man who had no consideration for women. He threw in her face the fact he slept with whores, and there was no filter between his brain and mouth.

"There are a lot of memories here."

The elevator dinged, and the doors opened. She followed behind him as he moved to the end of the hall and turned left. He stopped and used another key to get into his apartment.

Henry dropped her bag on the floor and allowed her inside.

Staring around the space, she stepped into his world. He closed the door, and she wasn't afraid. She was learning fast that Henry wasn't the kind of man she first thought. He was a killer, but he wouldn't kill just anyone.

"This is going in my safe." He pulled her gun from his back.

"Hey, I need to learn how to use that."

"I'll teach you how to use it soon, but I'm not doing it while you're hurting." He disappeared, and she stayed still within his space. She didn't know what to do. This was his apartment, not hers.

"There, I feel happier having you here with your gun safely away."

"You're overreacting."

"I'm not. You're completely insane. I can't believe you bought a gun and don't have the first clue how to use it." He picked up her case. "Come on, I'll show you to your room."

She moved behind him looking at everything she saw. His apartment was clean, completely clean, but then she remembered there were cleaners who took care of the apartment.

The walls were white, and he had black furniture. From what she saw his space was normal for life as a bachelor. Nothing was out of place, and there was nothing personal to the rooms.

"This is my room. There is a connecting door between the two rooms, but you don't have to worry about me hurting you or taking advantage."

She glanced down at her awful clothing. No, she didn't imagine he'd take advantage of her. He'd need to be attracted to her, and there was no chance of that.

"Hey, what's the matter?" He tilted her chin back.

"Nothing. I know you won't take advantage." She tried to pull away, but he wouldn't let her. Lydia liked the touch of his fingers way too much. He made her think about how good it would feel to have those fingers playing with other parts of her.

"You're thinking something completely different from what I am," he said.

She shook her head. "It's okay, really, I understand."

He pressed her against the wall, locking his fingers with hers and keeping them by her side. "No, you're not thinking right, baby. The only reason I won't be taking advantage of you is because of your cracked ribs. I can't bear the thought of causing you more pain, and I will never hurt you."

Lydia went to say something else to dispute his claims.

"The shit I said to you on that night was exactly that, shit. I don't think you're fat, and you're exactly what I love about a woman." He released her hands and slid his own across her waist, over her rounded stomach. "I spend too much time imagining these curves and how you'd look on my bed."

She stared up into his eyes, drawn to him.

He pressed closer until his lips were a breath away from her. "I stay away because I know you can do a hell of a lot better than me or Darren."

His words shocked her. She didn't know he thought that much about her, and yet, he did. He pulled back.

"It's time for you to get some rest."

Henry placed her case on the floor then headed toward the door. "Leave your clothes. I'll help you with them in a little while." He closed the door behind him leaving her alone with her thoughts.

There was far more to Henry than she first realized.

Chapter Six

Henry finished putting away the groceries he'd gone to get as Lydia made her appearance. She was no longer dressed in Donna's maternity wear but in a pair of duck pajamas. Her hair was bound up on top of her head, and she rubbed her eyes as she walked out of her room.

"That bed is the best thing I've ever slept on." She didn't stretch or complain.

"How are you feeling?" he asked, watching her move as she took a seat at the kitchen counter. She'd been out for most of the day. He'd taken the time to clean and go shop. For the longest time he'd not been in this apartment, and he didn't like the feelings it was all inspiring.

When he and Caleb went into business and had a successful, profitable year with Ecstasy along with their less legal businesses, he'd bought this place.

The entire apartment building was pure luxury, something he'd never lived in. His mother had been a whore and his father a pimp or a john. Growing up in the gutter he was used to being looked down upon. When he got older he'd learned to use his fists to get what he wanted. Fighting illegally got him away from his mother and the place where he grew up.

Meeting Caleb had been brilliant. They'd clicked instantly, neither wanting to spend the rest of their lives together fighting.

"I feel better, much better."

One of her hands went to her bound ribs.

"You don't have to worry. I'm not going to kick you out on the streets if you're feeling better." He flicked the button on the kettle and turned back to gaze at her.

She looked so beautiful even without all the makeup she usually wore.

"I don't know what to say to you," she said.

"There's nothing you need to say."

"You're like two different people, one that I like and the other that you need to be for the rest of the world to see." She held her hands together in front of her. "Which one's the truth?"

Neither was the truth. When he was around Lydia he wanted to be what she deserved. He was so used to women taking his money that he really didn't know what to say to her.

Taking down a couple of cups from the cupboard, he started to make them both a coffee. The last time he'd been cruel to her he lowered his guard and they ended up getting taken. He didn't want to put her in danger again.

"Henry?"

"Nothing is real. Okay. I'm being considerate." He placed a cup in front of her.

Before she woke up, he'd gone into the room where he'd packed away all of his hobbies years ago. The business had come first above anything else.

The scars on his face had been the start of his spiral, and then something had snapped inside him and he hadn't come back to this apartment.

"Something is real. This place, I wouldn't expect it from you. You've never given me any sign that you're not a, erm, a criminal."

He lifted the cup he was holding to his lips and took a large swallow of the steaming liquid.

"All you've ever talked about is whores and being crude." She stopped talking. He saw her cheeks were bright red, and he felt bad.

"I'm not anything important, baby. This place..." He didn't know what to say. There were no lies inside this space. "When I bought it I was young, naive, and an idiot. I didn't expect to become who I am now."

"What did you expect?" she asked.

"I don't know what I expected. I guess I wanted something a little different."

"What do your parents think of who you are?"

"My parents don't know who I am and don't give a shit. Mother was a whore, and my dad was a pimp or a punter, I don't know." He kept drinking the steaming liquid while staring at her.

Her lips were calling to him with the way she kept nibbling her bottom lip. He wanted to kiss her earlier. The need to kiss her lips and touch her was like fire in his blood.

"I'm sorry to hear about that."

"Shit happens."

"Do you want kids some day?"

"No. I live in a shit world with shit people. I don't want to bring anyone else into my world." He'd seen how precious Luke was to Caleb. There was no way he'd ever be able to handle the stress of keeping his son or daughter protected against everything. He didn't know how Caleb was handling the stress. "What about you?"

"I wanted kids, but now I don't think I'll bother." She sipped at her drink.

For the longest time neither of them spoke. He didn't like the silence. This woman had him all in knots just by her company alone.

"Did you go shopping?" she asked, several minutes later.

"Yeah. There was nothing in the house. I didn't take long. You were out of it for quite some time."

"I can't believe I slept like that. I don't recall ever being so tired before in my life."

"It happens to the best of us."

Who was this man that was taking over his body? Lydia clearly didn't know what to make of him and neither did he. Fuck, he was all over the place. "So, I rented a couple of movies for us tonight. I didn't know what you liked, so I just went ahead and rented what I wanted to watch."

"Okay, that's fine by me. I don't really watch much television anyway. I'm more of a cook and baker." She finished sipping at her drink.

He couldn't take his eyes away from her.

"Go and sit down." He moved around the counter to get the television set up. This was all new territory to him, taking care of someone else. He helped her to get settled, propping her up with a couple of pillows. She didn't argue with him as he moved her to help get her comfortable.

When she was comfortable she let out a sigh. He stepped back, setting up the movie. Sitting beside her, he lifted her feet onto his lap and simply sat back and watched the screen. Neither of them spoke, and he was shocked by how much he liked the peace of being with her.

"What movie did you put in?"

He mentioned the latest action movie that had a lot of gun fights and explosions but not a lot else.

She didn't say anything else as they both relaxed while the time passed.

Toward the end of the movie his cell phone went off. Seeing it was Caleb calling him, he made his excuses and headed toward his bedroom.

"What do you have for me?" he asked, turning the phone on.

"They're part of Drake Stone's operation. He's trying to get men we don't know to make deals that will help him get on the inside."

Henry cursed. "I was right."

"Yeah, you were. Elijah is pissed, and he wants to take Drake and the men out. They may have come across as a shit operation, but these men are the real deal, Bill and Leon. They've got a reputation for being able to hide. They're both wanted men and have avoided the law."

"I don't give a fuck about Drake. I want the men who hurt me and Lydia. I'll find them. No one can hide for long."

"This isn't about you. You've got feelings for Donna's friend," Caleb said.

"I've not got any feelings. Look, I was a bastard to her, and because of what I said to her, she ended up in trouble. I'm not going to let it happen again."

Caleb was silent for several seconds. "I'll let Elijah know."

"He can have Drake and the rest. I'm not interested in them. The only people I want are the ones who thought they could take us without any consequences. I won't let it stand. Professionals they may be, but they've never had me looking for them."

"How is babysitting duty?"

Getting to his feet he looked toward the sitting room. Lydia was leaning her head against the back of the sofa. She held the remote in her hand and was flicking through the channels.

"It's fine."

"Good. Donna's worried about her staying with you. I've told her there's nothing to worry about. I remembered you before when you actually cared."

"I don't care," Henry said, lying.

He cared way too much, which was why he tried to keep as far away from temptation as possible. Lydia was a big temptation to him, one that he'd been denying himself for some time now.

"You can lie to everyone else but not to me. I'm not in the mood to be lied to. We both know how attached you become to others."

"I've got to go."

"I'll let you know when Elijah wants to take out Drake once and for all."

"Sure." He hung up the phone and stood watching Lydia. It was about time they took Drake out. The little fucker didn't know when to stay away. He was pissed off that the little shit had gotten to him. It wouldn't have happened if he'd not been so fucking jealous of that bartender eyeing up his woman.

Fuck, when had she become his woman?

He didn't know when he'd gotten to thinking about her as his.

She turned her head to glance back at him. "Is everything okay?"

"Yeah, Donna's worried about you being alone with me."

Lydia smiled. "She thinks you hate her."

"I don't hate her. I just don't think she's right for Caleb."

"He loves her."

"She's too sweet, and he's anything but sweet. This life is not for the easy loving people." He rubbed a hand down his face. "Are you hungry?"

Lydia nodded.

"Donna's wrong."

"What do you mean?" she asked.

"I don't hate Donna. I just don't think this life is the right one for her." He headed toward the kitchen, pulling out the packet mixes he'd picked up at the store.

"What are you cooking?" She walked slowly toward him, taking her time to get there.

He lifted the packet and gave it a shake. "It's the best I can do."

"I don't mind."

"Can you cook?"

"Yeah, it's probably the only thing I can do well. Maybe when I'm better I can treat you to a dinner."

"I'd like that." He liked the idea of that way too much.

Henry felt her gaze on him as he moved around the kitchen. It took him several minutes of opening cupboards and drawers to find the saucepans.

Lydia giggled as he struggled to find what he was looking for. By the time he was set up, they were both chuckling.

What was worse, he couldn't remember when he'd had this much fun. What had happened to him in the last few years? It felt like he was unrecognizable. Lydia was making him see the difference in his life. The whores were a convenience, and his life had become one long line of conveniences.

Once he finished making their food, he sat beside her at the counter, staring at the mess he'd made of his kitchen.

"I've not had this much fun before in my life, thank you." She touched his shoulder, and he didn't know why but Henry felt like a changed man.

There was no way he could go back, not after this.

The whores were gone, finished, and so was hiding. He wasn't going to hide from his life anymore, and it was all because of Lydia.

****

One week later

She'd been confined to his apartment for the last week, but instead of being close to losing her mind, she was thriving in the space. Henry had bought her several cookbooks along with a few of her pans from her apartment. When he'd turned up with her equipment she'd been so surprised and had hugged him. Her ribs were feeling much better, and so he was letting her do odd jobs around the apartment. He wouldn't let her overexert herself, which she liked.

Henry still made food for them, but he allowed her to play at baking cookies. She was sure in the week alone she'd put on over a pound of weight with how long she'd been sitting on the sofa. He left every day to go to work. She didn't know if he was going to the women he liked to pay for, but she never called him out on it. The way he'd taken care of her she had no reason to complain. Neither of them had taken it any further. She was scared of what his almost kiss meant.

Standing at the counter she stared into the fridge. It was past five, and she didn't want to wait around for him to come home to eat. Deciding to surprise him, she grabbed the fresh ingredients she needed, and she took her time to make them some chicken with marinara sauce and pasta.

Her ribs were a dull ache. They no longer hurt so much.

Thirty minutes into cooking she heard the door open and close. Henry appeared in front of her. "What the hell are you doing?" he asked.

"I wanted to make you dinner." She stood holding the spoon as he glared at her. His bruising had almost disappeared. Lydia had looked in the mirror to see her bruise fading but not totally gone.

"You're supposed to be resting, not hurting yourself. If you keep this up, you're not going to get better but worse." He dropped his keys onto the counter. Looking at the stove where her labor of love was bubbling up, Lydia felt tears fill her eyes.

"Okay, I'm sorry." She placed the wooden spoon on the counter and was about to step away.

"Fuck, are you crying?"

"I'm not crying." She was close to crying, but she wasn't actually crying.

"Why are you crying?" She looked up as he rounded the kitchen to get to her. He reached out, cupping her cheek.

"I told you, I'm not crying." She made to move away, but he tightened his hands around her chin, stopping her. Lydia didn't want to move away from him.

"You're crying. What did I say to upset you?"

"Why are you angry at me for making dinner for us both? It's late, and you've been to work. I wanted you to look forward to something to come home to." She pointed at the dinner bubbling away. It would be another half an hour before it was done, but it would have been so worth it. Chicken with marinara was one of her favorites. She didn't know why she was so sad about the fact she didn't get what she wanted.

Life sucks sometimes, but this wasn't a problem with life. This was because Henry didn't want her cooking in his kitchen. Great, the very thought of him not wanting her around just depressed her more. He allowed Donna to visit with Luke, but her friend rarely stayed too long.

"You made this for me?"

"Who else would I cook for? I wanted you to have something to look forward to, and yet you're acting like I did something wrong. I just wanted to do something nice for you." She stopped talking to suck in her lips. Her emotions were running away with her. "Forget about it. I won't invade your kitchen again."

He cursed. "I mess up all the time. I don't care about you using my kitchen. What you're cooking, it smells amazing. Your ribs are not better, and I don't want you to overexert yourself."

"I'm feeling better."

"I know, but I don't want you to go back a step. The reason you're here is because of me."

She frowned. "No, it's not. I'm here because some asshole used me as a punching bag. It's not your fault." Over the last couple of days she'd come to realize that Henry wasn't like how she thought he was. There was so much more to him than being a crude man who was gun happy.

He tilted her head back, stroking his thumb across the fading lines of her bruise. The pain in his eyes was so clear to see that he took her breath away. "Every time I look at you and I see these I'm reminded that those bastards are still out there."

Lydia gripped his hand. "Don't do that, Henry. You'll get them when it's time. You don't need to rush to find them for me."

"I promised you I'd kill them."

She'd been surprised when she hadn't developed nightmares the first night she was here. Any time she got scared she would wake and think about Henry and all of her problems would fade away.

"I believe you."

"You're not afraid?"

"Of you? No, I'm not afraid." She licked her lips then glanced down to stare at his lips. What would it feel like for him to kiss her?

"You've changed since last time?"

"A lot more is going on now. I wasn't afraid of you last time. I didn't know you. I don't know you now, but what I do know is you won't hurt me." She reached out to touch his scarred cheek. He didn't pull away from her, and she traced the outline of the mark on his skin.

"This tells me a story. It's not a nice story or an easy one, but there's more to you than meets the eye, Henry."

"What are you doing to me?" he asked.

She released his cheek and covered his hand that held her face. "The exact same thing you're doing to me." Lydia dropped his hand down to her breast. Her heart was racing, and she couldn't stop what she wanted. She wanted to have his hands all over her body, to feel what he was doing to her. He cupped her breast, and she released a breath. "This is what you do to me every time we're together. I can't stop thinking about you." This was the first time she'd ever put herself out there with a man. She never allowed herself to get too close. Most of the men she'd been with had used her for sex and money. Darren had only used her because she'd been convenient as she had a place to stay. God, when was she going to stop falling for losers who only wanted her for what she could give them?

Stepping back, she shook her head. "I'm sorry. I shouldn't have done that."

With her humiliation complete she wanted to do nothing more than go and hide underneath a rock.

"No." He caught her hand and eased her back against him. She stared up into his eyes.

"What are you doing?"

"What I've been imagining for so damn long. I can't go another second until I know exactly how you taste." He dropped his head toward hers, and before she could stop him, his lips were on hers.

She moaned at the harsh feel of his thin lips against hers. There was nothing gentle in his kiss, yet it was something she craved. Sinking her fingers into his hair, she ignored the pain and wrapped both of her arms around his neck. This lust struck her hard whenever she was with him.

When she first saw him she'd been dancing with Darren. Henry had been in the VIP section of Ecstasy, but she'd seen him. Even from the distance, he'd pulled her attention. The man she'd been with was nothing like the scarred man sitting in the VIP section.

Even as he shot Darren, he'd not scared her. The situation scared her, not Henry.

His hands moved down to her waist, picking her up and placing her on the cleanest counter in his kitchen. She opened her legs wide so he'd have somewhere to sit between.

"Fuck, I can't get you out of my head." He broke the kiss only to press his lips down to her neck. "You always smell like lavender. I can't get the scent out of my head." She heard him inhale then exhale. "I could become addicted to your smell. So fucking addicted."

"You want me?"

"I've been trying not to want you for so damn long. I don't know what's real anymore." He drew back to stare back at her. She lost herself, cupping his cheeks as he stayed still. "What's this?"

"I want you, Henry. I just never knew how to tell you."

His hands moved up her ribs, and she couldn't help but wince from the pressure.

"Fuck, I completely forgot that you're hurt." He stepped back, stopping touching her instantly.

"I liked what we did." She hated the moment he stopped touching her. "I want to do it again."

"No, not until you're better. I can't—I've never been gentle, Lydia. I can't be what you want right now."

She nodded, licking her lips. He didn't realize how gentle he could be.

"I want to be something more to you. Could you get me down?"

His hands went under her ass, gripping her flesh as she lowered her back to the floor. The feel of his hands on her ass sent her pulse racing further.

"You're going to be a hell of a lot more to me." He tilted her head back. "You need to think about this long and hard, Lydia. Once I take you, you're mine. There's no backing down or pulling away. You'll be mine."

The ownership in his gaze sent a shiver down her spine. There was a hell of a lot more to Henry than he let anyone see.

"I want that, Henry." She'd never belonged to anyone in her life, and she wanted to belong to him.

He cupped the back of her neck. "You'll be mine. No hotel, no boys that are friends. You'll be mine."

She smiled. "It doesn't matter how many times you say it, Henry. I want to be yours. Truly, believe me when I say I want to be yours." She pressed a hand to his chest.

Henry stroked the back of her neck. The touch sent tingles throughout her body.

"Now, can I serve you some food, or are you going to keep being pissed at me? It'll be good. I promise."

"Feed me, woman."

Chapter Seven

Two weeks later

The last two weeks had been out of this world for Henry. He couldn't believe how happy he was and yet he'd not sexually touched Lydia, but that could all change within the next couple of hours. The doctor was scheduled to see her while he was out of the apartment. He stood in Elijah's warehouse with Caleb as they waited for Drake to spill the details of where the men were that Henry wanted.

They were leaving Elijah to torture the information out of him, but so far the bastard wasn't talking. He was either high or had a seriously high pain threshold.

"Donna wants you to come around to dinner," Caleb said.

"Not tonight. Lydia's seeing the doctor and I want to be alone with her."

"It's true then, you're going steady with a woman?"

Henry turned to look at his friend.

"The women at Ecstasy are talking. It has been over three weeks since you were last there, and every time you're at the club you never go near the back. I take it Lydia's taking care of your needs."

He smiled. "She's not. She's not taking care of anything." He still found his release in the shower by his own hand. She'd offered to help him out when she caught him fucking his fist. Henry refused. He didn't want her to touch him when he couldn't touch her.

"Wow, this must be a nice new change for you," Caleb said.

"It is."

"You look different. Donna mentioned it to me the other day."

"What do you mean?" Henry asked, glancing over at his friend.

The sound of Drake crying out filled the air, but it didn't stop either of them talking. Drake wasn't going to leave the warehouse alive. He'd been sloppy in his security. Usually Drake was surrounded by several large men carrying guns even when he was dealing with his women. For once Elijah's people had caught him alone, without anyone to help him.

"You're smiling. I've got to agree with her. This is how you used to be before the fighting and we got into this business. You know, before you were taken."

Henry folded his arms. Thinking about the time when he was taken wasn't the best for him. It was around the same time that he stopped going back to his apartment. The scarred face made it impossible for him to get away from the past. When he was around Lydia, he wasn't aware of the scars on his face.

"It's nothing."

"But Lydia's different. I see the man you once were. There's no way you can deny that."

Drake screamed as Elijah pulled out a nail. They were going back to historical torture methods. Henry had to respect the man.

"I'm not denying anything, Caleb. She makes me feel, and I like that."

"What about the other women?"

"They're done."

"Donna's worried."

"Have you turned into a pussy that answers to your woman, Caleb? Funny, you didn't strike me as the kind of man who took orders from a woman." Henry hated feeling like he was being observed under a microscope, and so far, Caleb and Donna were leaving him feel like a bug.

He turned to look at Caleb seeing the anger in his eyes.

"Shit, sorry, look, I don't want to argue or fight. You're my friend, and I appreciate your concern even though you don't need to. I'm not going to hurt Lydia. Tell Donna to stop worrying and to leave us to get it done."

Caleb nodded. "Fair enough."

Henry turned back to the action as Drake dropped his head sobbing.

"You may as well tell us where they are," Elijah said.

"Fuck off." Drake's voice no longer held the conviction that he was in control. He looked on the edge of death.

Elijah grabbed his hair, pulling the man's head back. Henry pulled his cell phone out of his pocket to see if Lydia had sent him a message. The screen was clear, and he quickly checked the time.

"You're going to put up a fight for no reason?"

"It's not for no reason," Drake said. Drool was pouring out of his mouth. His hands were a bloody mess.

"No?"

"We all know I'm not leaving this warehouse alive. Why should I give you anything? I'm dead anyway. It'll give me pleasure even in death to know you're going to suffer." Drake looked past Elijah's face to stare at him. "I heard Bill took a liking to your woman. It's going to be hard letting her out on her own with him waiting around to take her."

Henry tensed up, and Drake saw it.

"I knew there was more to her than a simple whore. Henry doesn't do whores. He fucks them at his club and never gets personal." Drake laughed. His teeth were decorated with blood, and there were several teeth that had been pulled. Elijah was one sick bastard. The art that he displayed with torture sickened Henry. He liked to pummel men and do the occasional torture, but there were limits even for him. Elijah was showing his sinister side. Henry wouldn't touch the mouth in any of his victims.

"Where are they?" Henry asked.

"You're going to have to wait to find them."

"This makes no sense. You don't get anything out of it. You're in pain."

"So, it's going to end soon. It makes no difference to me. I'm not giving you their location." Drake laughed, tilting his head back and coughing. "Why would I help you fuckers? We're enemies."

Elijah stood, and the chair he'd been sat on clattered to the ground echoing around the whole warehouse. He removed his jacket, then his crisp white shirt that he hadn't gotten any blood on. How many men had this fucker tortured?

"You two can leave. I'll take care of the rest."

Glancing at Drake, Henry almost felt sorry for him. He remembered Lydia's bruised cheek, and that took any kind of pity he felt for the bastard and knocked it dead.

"Call if he gives us anything," Caleb said.

"Will do. He's not going to be seeing death for some time."

They exited the warehouse and headed toward the car. Henry had picked Caleb up at the beginning of the day.

"Well, that was enlightening," Caleb said.

"I don't think it was enlightening, more like fucking frightening." Henry shuddered. "What the fuck do we know about Elijah?"

"That we shouldn't fuck with him. I tell you, I don't want to ever be in one of his chairs in that warehouse. Fuck that." Caleb pulled out a cigarette and lit it up. "You can drop me off at my house. I've got the rest of the night planned with Donna."

"Who's having Luke?" Henry asked.

Caleb groaned. "Okay, I'm going to spend the rest of the night with my woman and my son. When he's asleep I'll fuck my woman just the way she likes."

Henry chuckled. This was another reason why he didn't want kids. He was a selfish bastard and didn't want to share Lydia with anyone.

"Stop gloating. It doesn't look good on you."

"Actually, it does look good on me." Henry glanced over at his friend.

"Have you started painting again?" Caleb asked.

"No." Henry faced the road. No one but Caleb knew about his need to paint. This was insane for him to even be thinking about.

"Are you going to open up to Lydia?"

"I don't know, man. Shit, it's still in the early stages." And he'd not even looked at his paintings. They were stored away in the room that he kept locked.

Lydia hadn't asked about the room yet, which he was thankful for. He didn't know what he was going to say to her.

"Sorry. I didn't mean to bring it up."

"Yeah, you did." Henry ran a hand down his face keeping the other on the steering wheel. The past was still there, in the past. He didn't want to bring it into his future.

"Forget I mentioned anything. Send me a text or something to let me know if Lydia's okay. Donna will go out of her mind with worrying."

Nodding, he waited for his friend to be inside his home before steering out of the gated entrance. Glancing in the rearview mirror he saw the gates were closed before he even got a few feet. Caleb never risked his woman or his son's life. Could he do that? Keep Lydia and a child safe even in his world. The whole idea felt foreign to him. Why was he thinking about kids? He didn't want kids. The problem was Lydia. If she wanted kids, then so did he.

Their lives were dangerous, and Caleb employed two bodyguards to assist Donna when she wanted to go out. Henry didn't employ anyone as he could handle himself. They were getting deeper and deeper into this world, and it would only be a matter of time before he had to consider guards. Should he put a guard on Lydia?

Driving toward the center of the city took time. The roads were busy, and all he wanted to do was find out how Lydia was healing up.

He wondered what she'd have ready for dinner. Lydia could cook and not those packet mixes either. She cooked everything from scratch, and the food was to die for. He loved walking into the apartment with her cooking.

When he'd gone back to her apartment, he'd started packing it all away, bringing more of her stuff to his space. He hoped by the time she was fully healed she'd be all but moved into his apartment. In the trunk of the car he held another three boxes of her stuff. The landlord wanted rent payment by the end of the month. He hoped to have her apartment empty by that time and anything they didn't need put in to storage for her to decide on what to keep and what not to.

By the time he pulled up into the parking lot, it was dark, and he checked his cell phone to see no missed calls or texts. He didn't like this. The doctor should have given her the all clear.

Going to the trunk, he piled the three boxes onto each other. They were light, and it didn't take much strength to hold. He'd brought her cookbooks to the apartment earlier. Her collection wasn't large, and he intended to rectify that by buying her plenty of books. She could cook, and he'd never been interested in the kitchen.

Locking the car, he made his way over to the building, resting the boxes against the wall as he got into the building. He made his way over to the elevator, nodding at the man on the reception.

The ride up to his apartment was slow. He wanted to see Lydia to make sure everything was fine. Henry knew he should have stayed with her instead of going to the warehouse. He'd fucked up, and he wasn't happy.

The elevator opened, and he walked to his room. Fitting the key into the lock, typing in the number, the door opened and he walked into the apartment. He placed the boxes on the floor then closed the door.

"Lydia, I'm back."

He turned around and froze. She stood in a sheer white gown. No, there was no way white would reveal all that creamy flesh.

"Hey, Henry," she said. Her hands were rested at her chest. The robe went down to the floor.

What did he do with his hands?

"Hey," he said. His mouth was completely dry.
****

Should she have done this? Lydia saw him standing there, frozen. The doctor had come and gone, and she'd wanted to do something special for Henry.

Licking her lips, she glanced down at the floor feeling her confidence deflate. Is this what he wanted? On the same night where he warned her she'd be his, he'd taken her to his bed. Was this different?

"Hey," she said, back.

This had to be the worst seduction ever.

"The doctor cleared you?" he asked.

"Yes." She glanced up in time to see him checking out her body. "I didn't just want to send you a text."

"I can see that."

"You did say you were busy." She took a step closer, and his gaze fell to her exposed legs. Lydia took a step closer to him feeling the arousal grow within her body. After the doctor had given her the all clear with her ribs she'd spent the rest of the day preparing for Henry to come home. She soaked in the bath, taking her time to shave and wax delicate bits between her thighs. After she cleared the important parts of excess hair, she'd washed her hair, lathered her body, and then taken the time to dry naturally.

"I was never too busy to find out if you were okay."

"But if you found out I was fine you might not have given me the time to do this." She removed the robe for him to see her body naked. This was a huge step for her. The other men she'd been with she'd gotten naked in darkness and only been with them underneath the covers of the bed. He was the first man she'd ever stood naked before in full light.

"Fuck me." Henry reached out to hold onto the wall.

She rubbed her hands together in front of her. Her nerves were getting the better of her.

He took a step closer to her and then another. She stayed still until he was right in front of her.

"The doctor cleared you?"

"Yes. He told me he'd never had a patient who listened to him about rest."

Henry cupped her cheek. The bruise that had once decorated her cheek was faint. "You're more beautiful than I ever imagined."

She smiled up at him.

Swallowing past the nerves, she reached out to touch his jacket. "I put a casserole in the oven, and it'll keep for another few hours."

Running her hands up his chest, she opened his jacket and pushed it off him. He allowed her to remove the jacket then start at the top button of his shirt.

"You planned to seduce me?"

"I planned a lot of things for today, and I wanted it to be special." She removed his shirt seeing the scars that decorated his chest. "This is what happened when you were taken?"

"I was an ass, and I pissed off the man with the knife."

Tugging his hands from her face, she leaned in close and pressed her lips against each scar. Holding his hands at his sides, she licked her tongue from his nipple down to his navel.

"Fuck that feels good."

"I love the way you taste," she said, flicking her tongue along his chest.

She moaned then released his hands to go to the belt holding up his pants.

"No, I want to kiss you." He gripped her wrist, forcing her back up.

Henry sank his fingers into her hair, gripping the strands in his fist. She moaned as he tilted her head back.

She gasped as he pulled her close. The metal of his belt dug into her stomach. He slammed his lips down on hers, pressing his tongue into her mouth. She melted against him, loving the feel of his tongue inside her mouth.

He ran his tongue over her lips then slid into her mouth, plunging inside her.

She wrapped her arms around his neck, and he dropped one hand from her hair to cup her ass. Gasping, she drew back from his lips as his hands delved deeper, sinking into her pussy from behind. The position had her tight against him as he fingered her.

"So wet and tight. I can't wait to sink my cock into this sweet pussy." He removed his hands, and she watched him lick the digits into his mouth. The scent of her pussy wafted between them. Her cheeks heated with embarrassment by how wet she'd become. "And you taste better than I thought you would."

She rested her hands against his chest, watching as he took his time with each digit.

"You don't need to be embarrassed."

He started to walk her back. She didn't look behind her as he moved.

The coldness of the wall met her back. Within seconds he was on his knees and lifting one of her legs up and over his shoulder.

"You shaved your pussy all for me?"

She nodded, gazing down to see him on his knees before her.

He started to tease the lips of her sex, tracing over her mound then sliding between. The moment he touched her clit, she shook at the smallest contact. He knew what to do to drive her crazy with need.

"You're so responsive, baby." He pinched her nipple, and the scream she usually kept contained, released into the air.

The sound echoed off the walls. There was no time for her to come down from the pleasure as his lips circled her clit and started to suck inside his mouth. The intense sensation was more than she could stand. Crying out, she sank her fingers into his hair.

"No." He stopped licking her clit to grab her hands. "You're not the one in charge here. I am, and you keep your hands right by your sides."

She moaned as he attacked her pussy, flicking his tongue over the bud then sucking it into his mouth. Not one part of her body made any sense to her. She was his to do with as he wished.

He slid his tongue down to penetrate her cunt. She heard him moaning as he swallowed down her cream.

His fingers replaced his tongue, sliding inside her. "I'm not going to stop until you come all over my fingers. Come for me, Lydia. Let me feel this tight little cunt squeeze me."

She cried out, moaning as he was relentless in his torture. He wouldn't let her go and just kept licking her pussy. She was so close to the edge of bliss but couldn't seem to find that peak.

Henry plunged three fingers inside her and sucked on her clit. She came apart screaming his name as he gave her so much pleasure. He gripped her ass as her legs started to fail her.

Seconds later he stood up, staring into her eyes. "You've got the tastiest cunt I've ever had the pleasure of licking."

She watched him lick the cream from around his lips.

"Wrap your legs around me?"

"I'm too heavy."

"Put your legs around me, now."

Lydia didn't know if this was going to go how he imagined. She wasn't a light woman, but she did as he asked, wrapping her legs around his waist.

"Now, put your hands around my neck."

Biting her lip, unsure of what he actually wanted, she wrapped her arms around his neck.

The grip he had on her ass tightened. She squeaked at the slight pain, but suddenly she was no longer resting against the wall. He was carrying her toward the bedroom. The door was already open, and he dropped her to the edge of the bed.

"Keep those eyes on me."

She didn't drop her gaze doing exactly as he asked by keeping her eyes on him. Lydia liked his dominance and the way he ordered her to do certain things.

He gripped his buckle and started to release his pants. She'd never seen anything so sensual in all of her life. His body was large and muscular. She couldn't believe he'd carried her across his apartment without stumbling or breaking a sweat.

Lowering the zipper on his pants he slid them down until they fell onto the floor. At least, she thought they were on the floor but she couldn't see as she kept her gaze on his face.

The desire to look down at the evidence of his arousal was intense. She made sure to keep her gaze on his.

"I bet you'd have been the perfect pupil at school."

"Not at all." She smiled back up at him. "I was far from the best pupil."

"You'll do as I ask but not what a teacher wants?"

She shook her head. "I get something out of it here."

He stared back at her for several minutes. "You can lower your eyes."

Lydia kept her gaze on his face for a short time. When she could no longer stand to not look she dropped her gaze to the rock hard length of his cock.

Wow.

For the last three weeks she'd been wondering about his dick. Would he be long or thick, short or wide? She didn't know what to expect, but it wasn't the sheer perfection she saw.

He wrapped his fingers around the length, moving them up and down in his own rhythm.

"What are you thinking?" he asked.

She looked up at him. "You're, erm, bigger than I imagined."

"Is that a good thing that you imagined I was smaller?"

Lydia smiled. "No. Just think that you're always going to surprise me."

"Touch me." He reached for her hand and wrapped her fingers around the length of him.

The length of his dick was silky smooth to the touch but rock hard. She heard him hiss as she ran her hand up and down his length. The tip leaked pre-cum.

"Do you want to taste me?"

She'd never liked sucking a man's dick before. Henry was different. She wanted to give him the same kind of pleasure that he gave her. The feel of his lips and tongue on her body drove her wild.

"Yes."

"Open those plump lips and get ready to take me."

Chapter Eight

Lydia opened her lips, and Henry pressed the tip of his cock against her mouth. With her eyes still on him, she lowered her head and took him into the warm, wet heat of her mouth. Growling, he sank his hands into her hair needing to hold onto her hair to keep himself grounded. He watched her slide down his cock until he hit the back of her throat. She came up, flicking the tip with her tongue. Over and over she took him into her mouth, and her saliva coated his cock.

"Fuck, baby, you've got a perfect mouth," he said. She tightened her lips around his length, sucking hard. The suction almost had him coming. Tightening his fist into her hair, he cursed. "Be careful, baby. I don't want our first time to be inside your mouth."

She bobbed her head creating a rhythm that had him pulling out of her mouth. He couldn't stand the pleasure her lips were creating. Pushing her back against the bed, he followed her, opening her legs to reveal her creamy cunt.

Settling between her thighs, he gripped his shaft and pressed the tip to her entrance. Her cream coated the head, and he stared into her eyes as he slid deep inside her.

When she had a couple of inches of his cock in her pussy, he placed his hands on her hips then slammed the last several inches. She cried out, arching up on the bed. He sucked on the nipple she offered up to him, biting on the hard bud.

"That's right, baby. Come to me." He divided his attention between her two nipples, tonguing the hard buds.

"Please, Henry, move."

Rearing back, he stared down at where his cock was inside her body. The lips of her sex were open around his length, spread open wide to accept him. She looked so fucking sexy taking his cock. Pulling out of her, he watched his naked length covered in her cream reappear. It was like magic to him to witness the beauty of her accepting his shaft. When only the tip remained inside her, he stared into her eyes.

Holding onto her hips, he didn't break contact as he slammed deep inside her. She cried out, gripping his arms.

He felt every ripple of her pussy as he stayed still inside her. "How does it feel, baby?" he asked.

"Amazing. Please, don't stop."

"You want more of my cock?"

"Yes."

"Beg for it."

"Please, Henry, fuck me so hard. Give me your cock."

He slammed inside her over and over again. Her begging drove him harder. There was nothing more satisfying than hearing her pleasured cries. He pounded inside her, watching her cunt take every inch of him.

Her nails sank into the flesh of his wrists, holding him in place.

"Yeah, that's it, baby. Take my cock. You're soaking wet. Your cum's all over my dick." He couldn't look away.

The nakedness of his cock didn't bother him. In the last three weeks he'd made the doctor test him to make sure he didn't have anything. The results had come in a couple of days ago. There were no more women, no more whores. The only person he wanted in his life was beneath him taking his cock. The idea of kids no longer repelled him. Lydia made him want everything he'd denied himself since he'd gotten scarred.

Taking hold of her hands, he pressed them above her head, covering her body with his own. The hard buds of her nipples pressed against his chest sending his pulse racing.

"Give me those lips, baby."

Lydia didn't fight him, offering up her sweet lips. He slid his tongue into her mouth, deepening the kiss. She met him halfway, stroking her tongue with his.

He didn't stop thrusting inside her, going deeper than ever before. "Wrap your legs around my waist."

She did as he asked, and he slid deeper still. Kissing her lips, he slid down to her neck, sucking on her pulse. The moans coming from her lips turned him on even more.

"I'm never going to get tired of fucking you, Lydia. You better get used to having a cock inside you because it's always going to be mine."

"Yes, please." Her fingers sank into his hair, holding him tight against her.

Henry thrust inside her, watching the lust sparkle in her eyes as her cunt gripped him tight. There was no greater pleasure to be had than what she was giving him. "Fuck, I'm going to come."

There was no holding back. She was so tight and wet that he couldn't stop the pleasure. He thrust inside her a final time filling her with his spunk. Dropping his head to her neck, he thrust through the waves of ecstasy, feeling lightheaded when it was all over.

She kissed his neck, but he wasn't done with her yet. With his cock still inside her, he moved over, keeping her leg over his hip. His cock was flaccid, but he stayed inside her, not wanting to leave her.

Caressing down her body, he sucked on her nipple. He glided his fingers down between her legs. Finding her clit, he slowly stroked over the hard nub while also working her nipple. Her pussy came instantly alive, and he slowly thrust into her as he fingered her clit.

He pulled away to watch as her orgasm took over. She thrust onto his cock, tightening around him and washing his cock in cum.

When it was over, she collapsed onto the bed with a sweet smile on her lips.

"I take it you liked that, baby," he said, kissing her cheek.

She turned her head to smile at him. "Yeah, very much."

Henry pulled out of her.

"You didn't use a condom?" she asked, sitting up. He followed her gaze in time to see his own cum spilling from her nether lips. Never in all of his life had he seen something so amazing and erotic. He was rock hard at the sight alone.

"No, I didn't."

He saw the panic in her eyes. "Are you clean?"

"Yeah, I'm clean. I got the all clear from the doctor. I never went bare with any of the other women I was with. You're the first woman I've gone without a condom."

"What about pregnancy? I'm not covered. I'm clean, and I've always used condoms. I'm not on the pill."

"We'll deal with that when it's time."

"I don't want kids yet."

"Neither do I, but I wouldn't mind." He reached out to cup her cheek. "I'm sorry. I thought you'd have been on the pill."

Did he really? Did he want kids? In the past he didn't want them, but if Lydia decided she wanted them, he'd have them.

He'd seen how happy Caleb had become with children, but could he find that kind of happiness?

Lydia made him want to be different and to search for different things. This apartment was one of the changes he'd made. He no longer held an apartment in the old building underneath Caleb. This was his only place to stay. He didn't want the other life or the other women.

"I've not been with any other whores, Lydia. Our girls, I've not been near them since the night we were taken." He hated the fact he'd been with them prior to being a bastard to her. It sickened him.

"Not one?"

"You're mine, Lydia, and as far as I'm concerned, I'm yours." He touched her cheek, running a thumb over her lip.

"You're really something else." She cupped his hand, turning to lay a kiss to his palm.

There was so much he wanted to do to her.

"Are you mad at me?" he asked.

"For not using a condom?"

He nodded.

"No, not really. I'm not angry at you. I probably should be angry at you." She dropped her hands to her lap. "We'll need to go to the pharmacy, and I'll talk with the doctor."

"Shall we wait and see?" he asked.

"What?"

"I'll use condoms for the rest of our time together, but should we see if you're pregnant before taking that drastic step?"

"Are you sure?"

"Yes, I'm sure."

She didn't speak for several seconds. "Okay, if you're happy with that."

He was happy, and again he didn't know why.

****

Over the next week Lydia was on cloud nine. Henry was attentive and sweet to her. Since their first night it had only gotten better. He'd assigned a bodyguard to her whenever she wanted to leave the apartment. Her bruising had all but disappeared. There was no pain in her ribs, and she was good as new. Throughout the week they'd gone back to her apartment to collect the rest of her stuff. She should have seen the truth when Henry kept bringing her belongings back home every night.

He didn't want her working either. There were a lot of things he didn't want her doing. He'd ordered her not to shave her pussy again as he wanted that privilege.

She entered the apartment with Arnold following behind her.

"I can get home on my own."

"Until Henry gets back he wants you to have someone with you all the time," Arnold, the bodyguard assigned to her, said.

"It must be totally lame for you, following me around all day."

"Caleb and Henry are two of the most sought after men. It's a pleasure to be given this opportunity to work for them." Arnold closed the door, walking close behind her as she entered the kitchen. She'd been grocery shopping for their dinner.

"Really?"

"There are bosses who are not particularly fair. This job is a good one."

"How do you know Henry?" She didn't like having Arnold around and not talk to him. It seemed rude to her.

"I was a fighter. He and Caleb come to the fights and offer jobs to the men who are the most promising and discreet. They want men they can trust to get the job done."

Did she want to know any more about Henry's work? She knew he wasn't legal. The only thing that was legal about his entire operation was the club they owned.

"That's enough. I don't need to know anything else."

There was a buzz at the intercom. Leaving the kitchen, she walked into the hallway to find Caleb waiting to be let inside.

"Caleb? Henry's not here right now."

"I know. He's busy. I wanted to talk with you." She stared at him. This man did scare her. "Let me in, Lydia."

Arnold was home, so there was nothing Caleb could do. He was employed by Henry to keep her safe. She pressed the button and waited for the knock on the door. Arnold was stood in the hallway along with her.

He pushed her behind him as the door was knocked on. Caleb stood on the other side, raising a brow at Arnold.

"You can leave, Arnold. I've got it from here."

She didn't want Arnold to leave. Caleb looked at her, waiting.

"It's okay, Arnold. Caleb won't let anything happen to me." She turned on her heel and walked back to the kitchen. The only thing she wanted between her and Caleb was space.

The door closed, and she held her breath waiting for Caleb to come into eye sight.

When he did, she turned toward the fridge to finish putting away the cheese and cream.

"You and Henry," he said.

She glanced over her shoulder to see him stood waiting for her. He looked like he owned the place. Staring down at the cream in her hands, she didn't like the way he made her feel.

"What about me and Henry?"

"Is it serious?"

Lydia gave him her full attention. "It's serious to me."

"Henry is my friend, and we're business partners. What happens to him concerns me. You're a distraction. He's different since he's been around you."

"Isn't that a good thing?"

"He's determined to find those men who hurt you. This man is not the person I've come to rely on."

She tucked some hair behind her ear. "How is that being distracted?"

"He's missing other business. We're a team, and if he keeps going hunting, he's going to find what he's looking for and more."

Lydia saw he was concerned.

"Are you fucking with him because he killed your boyfriend?"

"What? No?"

"You don't strike me as a nice woman. Henry, he needs a nice woman to see past all the shit."

"What? You mean his scars?" She was getting angrier by the second. Caleb had no right to come here and accuse her of this stuff.

"You're in his apartment, and he's laid a claim to you. I don't like the vibe I'm getting from all of this."

"You think I'm using him?"

"He's got a thing for whores."

She threw the block of cheese at him. "First, I'm not a fucking whore. Second, Henry was the one who moved me into this apartment. I didn't suggest it once. And third, how fucking dare you. You don't know me or anything about me. I care about Henry. He means a great deal to me. I don't know if I love him yet as that's pretty fucking deep. I've never loved any man in my whole life. Henry, he's special, and I would never, ever, do anything to hurt him."

"Caleb, get the fuck out of my apartment," Henry said, rounding the corner.

Lydia gasped. She'd not heard him come into the apartment.

"Henry."

"Lydia, I want to apologize about my so-called friend," Henry said.

"I was worried about you, Henry. You're different. You're missing business while you're searching for these men, and it is going to put you behind bars."

"No, it's not. I'm not hurting anyone. Those men deserve to die, and I'm going to do it."

"You don't know anything about her," Caleb said.

She stared from one man to the other. Henry's hands were fisted while Caleb simply had his arms down by his sides.

"Neither did you when it came to Donna. All you saw was what you wanted. You wanted her, and I want Lydia. She's not using me, Caleb. I've told her to stop working. I already started moving her in with me before we were fucking. Get the fuck out of my apartment before I do something I might regret."

Lydia watched as Caleb stared down her man. She didn't want the two friends to argue over her.

"Henry?"

"No, Lydia. Stay out of it. He had no right speaking to you like that, and I won't have him doing it again."

"You're putting a woman first?"

"Didn't you when it came to Donna?" Henry asked.

She looked at Caleb when he made no sound of disagreement.

"Donna's my wife."

"Now she is. She wasn't when you first started out, so don't try and tell me otherwise. Donna was just another woman you fucked. Get out."

Henry and Caleb disappeared taking their argument with them. The door closed, and Henry reappeared in the kitchen. His hand went to the back of her neck. "Hey, baby, I'm really sorry about that."

"He's your friend. Doesn't he have a right to be concerned for you?" She didn't want to come between them, but Caleb's words were incredibly harsh.

"I don't give a fuck what he says. You're mine, and he doesn't allow me to say shit like that to Donna. I'm not going to let the bastard do it to you. I'll protect you."

He tilted her head back and claimed her lips. She melted against him as his tongue plundered her mouth. All thought of food disappeared as he pressed her up against the fridge. His hands moved down her body stopping at the bottom of her skirt. Henry lifted her skirt up. The tips of his fingers skimming over her thighs until one of his hands cupped her panty covered pussy. Henry growled. "What have I told you about wearing panties?"

She gasped as his lips moved down to her neck. He nibbled on her neck as he slid his finger underneath the edge of her panty.

Cream soaked the lips of her sex, and his fingers teased through her cum before sliding over her clit. She cried out as he pinched her clit then delved down to thrust inside her core.

"You're so fucking responsive, baby. Do you like my fingers in your cunt?"

Lydia stared into her eyes, never wanting to stop looking at him. The scars on his face didn't define him as a man. No, Henry, his actions that went unnoticed defined him to her. Behind closed doors he was the most amazing person she'd ever met.

"Yes."

"Do you want my cock?"

"Yes."

"Then get my dick out."

She tugged at his belt, working fast to free his cock from the confines of the pants that kept him.

Henry didn't leave her pussy, and she had to work around his searching hands.

"This is my pussy."

Every part of her belonged to him, and she had no interest in any other man.

"Please, Henry." She begged, needing to feel him inside her.

Seconds that felt like hours passed before she finally got his cock out. She stroked the entire length, smearing his pre-cum along the head.

"Fuck, I don't have a condom."

"I don't care. Please, Henry, fuck me."

He froze. His whole body tightened at her words. "Are you sure?"

"Yes. I trust you." She worked his cock until he batted her hand out of the way. He lifted her up ordering her to wrap her legs around his waist. What woman wouldn't love being able to be lifted? He pressed her against the fridge as one hand left her ass to take control of his cock.

Lydia paused as the tip of his large cock pressed against her entrance. She was so wet that he pushed the first few inches inside her with ease. They both groaned. The sounds echoing around the room as he sank inch by glorious inch inside her.

"Fuck, you're so fucking wet."

His curse words made her smile. Gripping his shoulders, she rested her head against the back wall.

On the last couple of inches he thrust hard and deep inside her making her cry out.

"That's it, baby. I'm deep inside you now. There's nowhere else for me to go."

Both of his hands returned to her ass, gripping the flesh.

Without the condom between them, she felt every pulse and jerk of his cock within her.

"No man will ever treat you like that again. You're mine, and I won't allow it."

She nodded, panting for him to move.

Slowly, he started to withdraw from her.

"Watch me, baby. Watch my dick covered in your cum."

Looking down she saw the rock hard length of him appear. His prick was slicked with her cum. He didn't give her a chance to admire the hard length as he rammed inside her.

Henry took control of the fucking, changing it up from a slow withdrawal to a harsh thrust. She loved the mixture of pain and pleasure and didn't want it to end.

"So fucking tight and hot." He pounded inside her. Sweat covered both of them. "Finger your pussy. I want to feel you come before I do."

She reached down between them, sliding her finger over her nub. The moment she touched herself it was an instant hit of sensation. She couldn't focus as he filled her to the brim.

"Come for me, Lydia."

From the look on his face, he was close to coming.

Fingering her clit she didn't take her time and just thrust herself into an orgasm that left her screaming. His fingers tightened on her ass to the point she knew she was going to have bruises from them.

Seconds later his cock tightened further, jerking as he spilled his cum inside her. He growled against her neck. His hot breath brushed across her pulse.

Closing her eyes, she wrapped an arm around his back, holding him close.

"I never want to let you go," she said, speaking the words softly.

She opened her eyes when she felt him move. Henry was staring at her, his face completely closed off.

"I'm not going anywhere, Lydia."

Chapter Nine

Leaving Lydia asleep in bed, Henry moved out of the bedroom to stare at the door that he kept locked. He'd not been inside that room in over ten years. It was time for him to go back inside. The key lay in his hands, and he took several steps toward it. Inserting the key into the lock he opened the door. There was no creak or waft of cobwebs. He'd given the key to the cleaning crew for them to come in and dust so there were no shocks for him as he looked around the room. Everything was under old blankets and covered. The windows still sparkled letting him know the cleaning had been consistent. He stood looking at the room he'd first installed when he bought the place. There was a section in the center of the room for what he wanted to display so he could paint. There were several canvases all around that were blank. He'd not had much time to actually paint anything of real substance. Pulling the blankets off the equipment he returned the room to its former glory. He threw the piles of cloth into the corner, keeping it out of the way. Everything was packed away, and he started opening drawers arranging it all back into its place.

The canvas on the easel showed the fruit bowl he'd been painting when his life changed. Sitting on the stool, he stared at the painting seeing how impersonal it was.

There wasn't anything personal in this room. He'd liked to paint and draw for as long as he could remember. When he got his own place that he knew wouldn't be broken into he'd invested in what he enjoyed.

Removing the fruit canvas, he replaced it with a clean one and simply stared at the sheet.

Minutes passed, he didn't know how many, and yet he still couldn't bring himself to draw or paint anything. The first step was complete in getting him into the room.

"Hey," Lydia said.

He turned to see her wrapped in the blanket. She leaned against the doorframe staying out of the room. Her shoulders were bare, and her brown hair cascaded all around her. She looked tired and well fucked.

"Hey," he said, staring at her. She was a beautiful woman, and she was all his.

"You were gone, and I didn't like it." She stayed out of the room.

"Why don't you come inside?" he asked, wanting her beside him.

"Are you sure? This place was locked up tight. I guessed it was your space."

He smiled. "You can come in providing you drop the blanket."

She tilted her head to the side, looking so damn cute as she did.

The blanket dropped, and she walked into the room, naked.

His cock hardened at the sight. He was naked as he'd not taken the time to actually put on any pants. Taking hold of her hand, he tugged her down onto his lap.

"You paint?"

"I used to paint. I don't anymore."

"Why not?"

He stroked her thigh, loving the feel of her smooth flesh.

"Shit happened, and I didn't want to do this anymore. I'm not the same man who bought this apartment."

"Why not?"

He shook his head, not wanting to remember the old memories.

"Don't lock me out. Talk to me. I want to know everything." She took hold of the hand stroking her thigh, locking their fingers together. "I'm not going anywhere."

He blew out a sigh. "I was on a job with Caleb. We were first starting out and making a mark for ourselves. One of the drug lords didn't like us making a mark. We were two bastard fighters who didn't know our place. Anyway, one night I was stupid and lured back to a woman's place. I didn't know she was a whore at the time, and I was taken from behind. I didn't even see it coming. When I woke up, I was chained up in a warehouse." He stopped. She didn't need to know everything that happened. "I was tortured for information. It took Caleb a good few hours to find me, and in a couple of hours they can do a hell of a lot of work. I was messed up, and something changed. When I healed and was able to move around. I came back here only to find that I was different. This place didn't hold anything for me. I know it's fucking ridiculous, but I no longer wanted to be here."

"Has it really been that long since you've been here?"

"I came here and knew I couldn't stand it. I packed everything away and rented an apartment in the same building as Caleb. I paid for the cleaners to keep an eye on it while I was away. When I brought you here, it was the first time that I came here since I closed it up. I packed up everything that I wanted, and everything else I left behind."

"Are you going to paint?" she asked.

"You're not going to call me names for leaving this place behind?"

"Why would I do that? You were hurt and didn't want to come back here. I can understand that even if this place is awesome." She kissed his cheek, resting against his chest. "Will you paint something for me?"

"You want me to paint?" He'd entered the room getting past that first step. The last thing he anticipated was to actually paint something. Henry didn't want to say no to her.

"If you're not ready you can tell me no."

He stared down at her, and what he saw in her eyes scared him. She cared about him as he heard her telling Caleb that she did have feelings for him. It wasn't love, yet from the look in her he knew it was close.

"I'll paint, but you're going to have to be the person I paint."

She pulled away. "You want to paint me?"

"Yeah. You're the only person I want to paint. Will you be a model for me?"

He saw she was struggling.

"If you want me to be a model? Are you sure about this? You could get a lot of other people willing to sit for you."

"The only woman I want to draw is you." He dropped a kiss to her lips. "Let me draw you."

She rolled her eyes but stood. "Okay, but you've got to promise me you won't show anyone else."

"I promise. The only person who'll get to see this is me."

Lydia nodded. "Where do you want me?"

Henry didn't want her in this room. There was nothing special about the room, and when he painted he wanted Lydia to feel special.

"Go back to bed. I'll grab what I need." He watched her leave the room. Grabbing the easel and the canvas he made his way into the bedroom. She lay on the bed with her knees drawn up to her chest.

"Stop worrying," he said.

"I don't know what to expect."

"Don't expect anything. I'll be back in a minute." He walked back into the store room selecting the colors he needed. Once he had everything, he made his way into the bedroom. Staring at Lydia, he started to direct her to how he wanted her to lie. He had her lying across the bed, staring at him with a smile. She was on her stomach, showcasing that wonderful curvy ass. One of her hands was in her hair, resting her head while the other was flat on the bed.

He took his seat behind the canvas. For several seconds he simply admired her frame. She was so tempting to him. His cock was long, hard, and pulsing with need to be inside her.

"You don't have any idea how tempting you look."

"I can see you like it." Her gaze wandered down his body to rest on his large shaft.

"Don't worry, baby. When I've finished drawing you, I'll take care of your other needs." They'd not used a condom all night, and he was happy about that. He didn't want anything to be between them.

Picking up a pencil, he started to outline her body. It was late, but he wasn't leaving her alone tomorrow. He wanted to spend the whole day with her. The last couple of days all he'd done was search for Bill and Leon with no luck. The men could wait while he was with his woman.

"You're going to have to talk with Caleb again soon," she said.

"I only kicked him out of our apartment a couple of hours ago. I'm sure he'll be okay to wait a little longer until I'm ready for him."

She shook her head. "You're best friends and have been through so much together. Please, don't let him hate me. He's going to think I'm poisoning you against him or something."

He chuckled. "Baby, it's going to take a hell of a lot more than a few choice words from you to turn me against Caleb."

"I don't know how he thinks. I just want things to go okay. I'm friends with Donna."

"I'll talk to him. He better not say shit about you, otherwise my fist is going to have a meeting with his face."

"You're threatening violence again."

Henry glanced at her smile. "Get used to it."

He wasn't going to change what he did for a living. There was no way he'd ever afford something like this if he looked for a real job. He didn't have the qualifications to get on the straight and narrow.

"I'm not asking you to change, Henry. You've stopped screwing around with whores. If you were still with them, then I'd kick your ass. You're not, and I'm fine with that."

"Good. I'm not going back to the whores. I'm done with them." He was a one woman man.

****

Lydia blew out a breath, feeling overly exposed. Henry rarely spoke only to mumble something here and there. She didn't know what time it was, but it had to be early in the morning. He hadn't stopped with the pencil, and she didn't see him stopping anytime soon. She loved watching him. Every now and then he'd appear around the canvas looking over her body, caressing it with his gaze alone. She was so hot and horny from the looks he was sending her way.

Earlier, she had lied to Caleb. She was falling in love with Henry. Ever since she first met him over a year ago he'd intrigued her. The feelings he inspired inside her hadn't gone away. Every time she saw him, she'd been drawn to him. It wasn't the scars on his face or the malice in his eyes, it was the man himself. She'd seen past the scars and wanted to know the man deep inside. What she saw took her breath away.

He wasn't just some brute who used his fists. This apartment was one of the things that showed a side to him not many people knew. Henry had bought an apartment in the city that was known for its security. He didn't want to be looking over his shoulder as he slept. The whores were merely easy sex. He'd been hurt so many times by women turning their nose up at him. It was sad, harsh, and it had broken a part of him. He clearly didn't believe he was worth loving or even liking. The painting was another element. This entire life had been bought when he had big plans and intended to explore those plans. Someone had taken that life away from him.

"The man who gave you those scars and took this world away from you, is he dead?" she asked.

Her words made him tense.

Henry's eyes appeared around the canvas as he stared at her.

"Yes, Caleb and I hunted them all down and killed them. We never leave our enemies alive."

"Is that another reason you want to hunt the men who took you a few weeks ago?" she asked.

"No. I want to kill those bastards because they hurt you and treated you like a whore. You didn't deserve it." The menace was back once again making her shiver. "I'm not having you scared to walk the street."

"I'm not scared. You have Arnold looking after me."

"Okay, I'm not going to be happy until I know they're dead."

She was scared. There were times when she saw men in hooded jackets, and she wondered if Bill or Leon were behind them.

"Does that scare you?"

"No." She was being honest. Henry had never physically hurt her. "I'm getting tired."

He disappeared behind his canvas. Seconds later he stood up. "I can call it a night, but first I want to take a picture." Henry grabbed his cell phone from the drawer top and aimed it at her.

"You better not share this with any of your friends."

"There's no way I'd share you with my friends." He placed the phone from where he got it and carried the canvas away.

"Hey, don't I get to see the masterpiece?"

"Not until it's done."

He left her alone, and she stayed in the position he left her. When he came back into the room, his cock was rock hard, pointing at her. He moved toward her feet and slid between her legs, covering her body.

His hand moved to his cock. "Push your ass up."

She was soaking wet just from the evidence of his own arousal. Doing as he asked, Lydia groaned as he slid his cock deep into her. Both of his hands moved up her body. One cupped one of her breasts while the other moved the hair off the back of neck. His lips went to the back of her neck, and she cried out. He sucked on her flesh as he rode her hard.

The sounds of flesh hitting flesh filled the air, turning her on further.

"I could fuck you all day and night." He rested his face against hers. "Thrust up against me."

Doing as he asked, she thrust up to meet his cock. He sank in deeply with him going at her from behind.

"Who do you belong to?" he asked.

"You, Henry, I belong to you." He pounded inside her, and she loved the feel of him staking his claim over her. Henry stopped touching her breast and grabbed her hands. He kept them locked at the side of her head as he fucked her hard.

His hard body surrounded her, and she wouldn't have it any other way.

He swiveled his hips hitting a spot deep inside her. Several strokes over her g-spot and she came apart in seconds, crying out his name. Henry followed her, grunting out his release and sucking on her neck as he came apart.

When he finished, he collapsed over her.

Catching her breath, she enjoyed the feel of his weight over her.

"I wanted to do that ever since you dropped that blanket."

She giggled. "You were the one who wanted to draw me. I'd have happily have been fucking all night."

He pulled out of her, and they slid under the covers. His hand banded around her waist, pulling her close. She closed her eyes, basking in the feel of him.

"If we don't start using a condom I'm going to get you pregnant."

"I know." She ran her hands up and down his arm. "I like this."

"You do?"

"Yes, there's nowhere else I'd rather be, Henry. I love being your woman."

She nestled against him, feeling his cock thicken as she rubbed her ass next to his groin.

"Good because you've not got a choice. You're mine to keep now."

Opening her eyes, she stared across the room as a thought entered her head. "Henry, if you want me to start working, I will. I don't mind working."

"And I don't want you to. You're my woman, and I'm old-fashioned. I won't have you working. Ignore the shit that Caleb said. He doesn't let Donna work either, and he'd beat the shit out of me if I mentioned her being anything other than perfect."

"They're married."

"Do you want to get married for him to shut his trap? I'll marry you in a heartbeat."

She glanced over her shoulder to see he was being serious. "You'd marry me to stop your friend from saying nasty shit to me?"

"Of course."

Lydia pressed a kiss to his lips.

"Is that a yes?" he asked.

"Was that an actual proposal?" She was confused.

"Yeah, it was. I'm going to marry you at some point, baby. I don't know how many times I've got to say it, but you're mine. We're going to get married soon, and we may as well get to it now."

"Your romantic skills need a lot of work."

"Will you marry me?" he asked. He cupped her cheek. His thumb stroked over her lips. "I'm being serious, Lydia. I'm not going to have any other woman. The only one I want is you."

"How can you know?"

"I know." There was no hesitation in his words.

"Yes, Henry, I'll marry you." She didn't want to be with any other man but him.

He pulled her close, dropping a kiss to her lips. "Now, it's time to go to sleep. We'll go hunting for a ring very soon."

"You don't want to fuck again?" she asked.

Henry growled, nipping at her lips. She giggled but rested her head on his chest. He held her close, and there was nowhere else she wanted to be other than in his arms.

She was getting married. Life had never been better for her.

Chapter Ten

Several days later Henry was standing with Caleb inside Elijah's warehouse as they talked out distribution. The latest batch of coke had had several customers collapsing and being sent to the hospital.

"It must be something wrong with the batch," Elijah said, looking over the police reports their friend on the inside had given. There had to be some confusion as the women who collapsed showed signs of a date rape drug being present, too.

"This is your shit that you assured us was above board. I've got other suppliers who don't have their clients in the hospital or with elements of a date-rape drug. Anymore of this shit and I'll be investigated by the police," Caleb said.

"What about Richard?" Henry asked. He still didn't like the seedy little bastard.

"He flirted with your woman, Henry. That's all. Leave him be."

"No, it's got nothing to do with that." Henry looked at Elijah. "We've been buying shit from you for months. All of a sudden we employ a guy, and we've got women, not men, women passing out in the club." The more Henry thought about it, the more it made sense. "What if it's not the coke?"

"What do you mean?"

Taking the file from Elijah, he flicked over the women. "They're pretty girls but not striking. We looked over this. What if he's giving them the rape drug as well as the coke? It's one woman a night, not many. I can tell you there's been a shitload of deals going in the club, and the whores have been snorting the shit out of it as well. Surely it has to be down to something else."

There was a reason he didn't like Richard, but he couldn't figure out what it was.

Caleb looked unconvinced while Elijah took the file back to read through.

"There's no sign of them ODing, only them being passed out. The date-rape drug is detected. She passed out and was unresponsive. The drug keeps women conscious without the ability to do anything. We passed them off into the ambulance without thought. What if he's done this before and we didn't know about it?" Henry asked.

"Fuck," Caleb said. "It all fits."

"What you've got to ask yourself is how many girls weren't packed away in an ambulance?"

Henry didn't like the way this was going. "Where's Richard now?"

Caleb glanced down at his watch. "He's in the club getting ready for tonight."

Pulling out his cell phone, he dialed Barry, who was one of the men who dealt with security and who they trusted. When they noticed the women passing out they'd asked for Barry to check security.

"Hello, boss," Barry said.

"What do you have?" Henry asked. For once he'd love for their job to be easy. He didn't like how one of their staff had been taking advantage. This was his world, and he took care of it.

"It's not good. I recognized three women on camera who'd passed out. It was busy on a Friday night so I didn't get to them. On the camera it shows Richard carrying them out looking like he's helping them. I've just visited one of the women who was taken. She's not been back to the club since." Henry stared at his friend, knowing he wasn't going to like it. "She was raped by Richard and threatened if she ever said anything he'd slit her throat. He worked for Drake, Henry. We fucking missed it. His references were all clean."

Cursing, Henry rubbed at his eyes. "Make sure she's compensated and let her know the bastard will never hurt her again."

Hanging up the cell phone, he conveyed the information to Caleb.

"We're going to the club," Elijah said. "I deal drugs for the high not to abuse women. I want this bastard taken care of. I've got a fifteen year old daughter. I'm not having a monster on the streets."

Henry hadn't known Elijah had a daughter.

"To some you'd be considered the monster," Caleb said.

"Don't care. I'm a monster with morals. I don't fuck with people who can't fuck back."

Leaving the warehouse, Elijah's bodyguards followed behind him. They travelled in Henry's car with Caleb sitting beside him and Elijah in the back.

"So, when is the big day?" Elijah asked.

He'd called Caleb up the following day after he proposed to Lydia to let him know he was going to marry her.

"We've not set a date," Henry said.

"Never thought I'd see the day that the deadly duet was married and settling down."

"Try it, Elijah. I wouldn't change Donna for anything."

"Married life is not for me. I'm happy with what I've got. I don't need a woman bitching at me."

"You've got a daughter. Shouldn't she have a mother?" Henry asked.

"My daughter is taken care of. Her mother is a first class bitch. Believe me, she doesn't need a mother.

I've got a nanny taking care of her." Elijah sat back, flicking through his phone.

They made their way across town toward Ecstasy.

Lydia was spending the day at the spa. Henry told her he was going to be at the club for most of the day and he'd see her later that evening. Henry was going to do more work on the painting while she cooked. She made him a better man, and he knew he was in love with her. From the first moment he saw her, he'd been caught in her dark brown gaze. He had been jealous of Darren who got to touch her when he couldn't.

She was his, and Henry didn't intend to lose her.

Entering the club, he heard a feminine whimper. He recognized that whimper. In the doorway he saw Arnold was on the floor with blood spilling from his side. The man was struggling to move, but no one was paying any attention to him.

"Let me go!" Lydia screamed.

The unmistakable sound of flesh hitting flesh tightened his gut.

"Shut your fucking mouth."

Caleb and Elijah were at his back.

"Is that Lydia?" Caleb asked, whispering the words.

He didn't say anything. Slowly, he entered the main part of the club. Richard was counting out money as Leon stood beside him. Bill grabbed Lydia by the hair and dragged her to her knees. The dress she wore was torn from her shoulders showing off the yellow lace underwear he bought her.

Anger consumed him as he took in the sight. The three men were standing there as if they owned this club. Pulling his gun from his hand, he clicked the safety off, drawing their attention to them. Elijah and Caleb also had a piece.

Lydia saw him. Tears fell from her eyes, but she looked so happy and relieved to see him.

"Henry," she said, trying to crawl to him.

"No, bitch." Bill yanked on her hair pulling a scream from her lips. It took every ounce of control for him not to simply fire at the bastard. They needed to know these three were the last men to deal with.

"What are you doing here, baby?" Henry asked.

"I wanted to come and see you. I brought you lunch, but those bastards ate it and shot Arnold. I had distracted him with a joke, and they pounced on him before he could do anything." She screamed as Bill pulled her to her feet, pressing a knife against her throat.

Pissed, he focused his gaze on Bill.

"She's not just a random whore," Bill said.

"You were working for Drake," Caleb said, interrupting everyone.

"Yeah, he got a kick out of the fact you gave me a job. He thought it was fucking hilarious," Richard said.

"Raping the women was just for kicks?" Elijah asked.

"It was easy and fun. I always like my women submissive." Richard pocketed the money.

"So we killed Drake leaving you three shit-heads to take his place."

"No one was watching, and there's more than enough room for all of us. We're not a problem," Leon said.

There was no way these men could take on the task of running a business. There wasn't even a brain cell among the three of them and Elijah said as much.

"You're all that's left?" Henry asked. He didn't look away from his woman, who had a knife pressed to her throat.

There was no way he'd live without her. He loved her with all of his heart, and the bastard holding her was going to die.

"We don't need bodyguards," Richard said, showing the fucker was dumb.

"Rule one, never give away how many people there are," Caleb said.

"Huh?"

"Lydia, baby."

"Yes?"

"Remember what I promised you?"

"Yes."

"It's going to happen now. Close your eyes if you don't want to see it." He fired his gun as Caleb and Elijah took out the other two.

Bill released Lydia, and she scrambled away from his hold. Henry advanced on the man, aiming his gun at Bill's head.

"What?" Bill asked, grasping his shoulder.

Henry hadn't had a clear aim while the bastard was hiding behind his woman. He had a clear shot now. Aiming his gun, he heard the other two men finish off Leon and Richard.

"You had no chance of winning. You touched my woman, hurt her, and now you're dead." He fired the bullet into Bill's head.

Dropping his weapon to the floor he turned in time to have Lydia in his arms.

"It's okay, baby. I'm here." He stroked her hair, trying to soothe her. He was shocked to see his own hands were shaking.

"I love you, Henry."

Her admission completely undid him.
****

Lydia sobbed against Henry's chest, telling him the truth of her feelings. "I love you so much."

"I've got you."

She pulled away to stare into his eyes. When she walked into the club to see Leon and Bill she'd not had the time to run away. They'd caught her before she got a chance to do anything. Throughout it all she knew Henry would come for her and she'd not been wrong.

He cupped her cheeks. "I love you, too, baby." He pressed his lips to hers, stroking his tongue inside her mouth.

Melting against him, she accepted his kiss. She made sure not to look at the evidence of the dead bodies.

Pulling away from the kiss, she kept her eyes closed against his chest.

"I'm going to get her out of here."

"Yeah, please, I don't want your lovey-dovey attitude to rub off," Elijah said.

"I'm sorry for treating you like shit," Caleb said.

She opened her eyes to see Henry's friend standing close. "It's okay. I know you were only taking care of him."

Running her hand over Henry's chest, she looked up at him smiling.

"What about me?" Arnold asked, groaning.

Henry kept her head locked to his chest.

"Go, we'll deal with him." This came from Caleb once again.

Henry held her as they made their way outside toward his car. Climbing inside the car, Henry took his seat beside her.

"Are you angry at me?" she asked as he drove toward their apartment.

"Why would I be angry at you?"

"I don't know."

Henry grabbed her hand. "I'm not angry at you. You didn't know they were there. I got you out of there because I don't want you to remember shit like that. I love you, baby. I promised to take care of you, and I failed."

"You didn't fail. How could you have known I was going to bring you lunch?" she asked, resting her head against the chair. Should she be freaking out over the fact she just witnessed three men get killed? When she thought about Bill lying dead, she was happy about it. "What did Richard do?" she asked. She'd been surprised to see the barman taking pills and cash from Leon. None of it made sense, and she told Henry what she'd seen.

He gripped the steering wheel a little tighter. "He was using the club to find girls he could rape."

She gasped. "Seriously?"

"Yeah. We just found out when we were talking with Elijah."

Lydia was pleased Richard was dead. They were three monsters.

Looking outside, she wondered if she would have been one of the women if it hadn't been for Henry.

Frowning, she turned back to him. "You love me?"

"You're only just hearing that now?" he asked, glancing at her.

"You said it though. You love me?"

"I do love you, baby." He squeezed her hand, bringing it up to his lips and laying a kiss on it.

Henry pulled up outside of the apartment. He removed his jacket and rounded the car toward her. Before she could protest he placed the jacket over her, covering her up.

Together they made their way up to his apartment. No one stopped them on their way. She snuggled against him, happy. He was in love with her, and she couldn't find fault with the world.

Once inside their apartment, he led the way down to the shower. Without saying a word, Henry removed his clothing then hers before tugging her into the small stall.

He wrapped his arm around her, holding her close.

"I'm completely in love with you, Lydia, and I'm not going to let anything else happen to you." He sank his fingers into her hair, making her breath catch. She didn't know how he did it, only that she never wanted him to stop.

"I love you, too." She ran her hands up his chest going on her toes. He gave her what she wanted. Moaning, she kissed him back.

The shower took over an hour as Henry showed her with his body rather than words how much he loved her. She'd never been fucked in the shower before, but Henry let her know what she was missing.

Afterward, he carried her to bed where she demanded he get an update on how Arnold was doing. She lay naked while he finished up the call. Running her hands over his back, she listened to him talk.

"Okay." Henry hung up the phone.

"Well, is everything okay?" she asked, concerned.

"Arnold is fine. He had to go to surgery to repair the damage the bullet made. In a couple of days he can go home. Caleb and Elijah dealt with the other three. It turns out Elijah's got some contacts that can dispose of dead bodies without a trace." He cupped her cheek. "Are you sure you can handle this?"

"I want you, Henry, all part of you." She kissed his hand. "I want to be your wife and give you children."

"Good, because there's no other woman I want more than you."

Epilogue

Six months later

"I'm getting a little creepy vibe here, Henry," Lydia said. He had a mask over her eyes as he escorted her into their apartment. They'd just been shopping with Donna and Caleb for their baby that was due in three months' time.

She touched her large stomach lovingly as Henry eased her into their apartment.

"You're going to love it. It has taken me long enough to get it done."

In the last six months they'd gotten married in a very simple wedding with only Donna, Caleb, and Elijah, along with his fifteen year old daughter, Casey and her nanny present. Lydia had loved it and would never forget how much she loved it.

"You're confusing me, Henry."

"Everything will be clear in a moment. Stop your fussing, woman."

He spent more and more time in his studio, which he rarely invited her inside. There was a time when she got jealous of the room as he seemed to be inside there more than with her.

Her eyes were still covered, and she heard the door close.

Caleb told her how much Henry had loved painting before he got the scars and stopped. All jealousy had evaporated, and she even started leaving food for him on a cart for him to eat. She took up cooking and knitting. For some reason knitting always soothed her especially when their son was kicking.

"Can I remove this blindfold yet? I'm freaking out a little."

"In a minute." He took her hands leading her further into the room. Blowing out a breath, she wondered what was going to happen when he stopped and removed the blindfold. Blinking, she stared into her husband's eyes. "Let me know if you hate it."

He stopped out of the way, and there was the painting he'd been working on. She was lying on the bed, staring at him with a smile on her face. Instead of looking frumpy and cellulite riddled, she looked sexy.

Pressing a hand to her mouth, she was taken aback by how he made her look.

"This is why I love you. You never fail to surprise me."

He wrapped his arms around her.

"This is what you've been working on?" she asked.

"Yes. I wanted to get it just right. I think I got it right, don't you?"

She spun around, wrapping her arms around his neck. "I love you so much."

"Baby, you've got no idea how much I love you, but I'll spend the rest of my life showing you and our children how much I do."

He claimed her lips, and Lydia was lost to everything else.

The End

www.samcrescent.wordpress.com

SAM CRESCENT

EVERNIGHT PUBLISHING ®

www.evernightpublishing.com